Bristol Short Story Prize Anthology

Volume Four

BRISTOL

First published in 2011 by Bristol Review of Books Ltd,
Unit 5.16 Paintworks, Bath Rd, Bristol BS4 3EH

1

ISBN: 978-0-9559555-8-7

Cover designed by Claire Shorrock

Layout designed by Dave Oakley, Arnos Design, Bristol

Printed and bound in Great Britain by Short Run Press, Exeter, Devon

www.bristolprize.co.uk
www.brbooks.co.uk

Contents

Introduction

Welcome to the fourth Bristol Short Story Prize Anthology. It has been another lively and exciting year and the Twittersphere and blogosphere, in particular, have been buzzing with praise for our 2010 anthology and the work we are doing. Our collaborations with school and university students in Bristol to promote short story reading and writing amongst young people continue to grow with schools producing adaptations and responses in different art forms to selected stories we have published.

The submissions for this year's prize show that the short story form has the unique ability to stun, move and delight readers in any number of ways and the broad range of work we received crossed the emotional spectrum from humour to tragedy and exhibited all facets of storytelling, exploring all manner of events, characters, social issues and moral dilemmas. In *No one Has Any Intention of Building a Wall* by Ruth Brandt, a human face is put on an event that had global reverberations. *Kitchen at the Lion* by Laura Windley takes the reader to a dark, near-future Britain. Genevieve Scott's *Ernie Breaks* is a tale of childhood tragedy told through a child's eyes.

It is, also, particularly pleasing that the competition appeals to established and new authors alike.

Judging this year's competition was no easy task and was not undertaken lightly. Every aspect of the stories was scrutinised. We went over every interpretation of the nuances within the stories with a magnifying glass at hand and some very long discussions ensued. Stories were read and re-read. Often a judge or two could be seen in a quiet corner of BSSP towers re-reading a story to make sure they had not missed any of the subtleties it contained.

This anthology comprises the 1st, 2nd and 3rd place submissions and the 17 other shortlisted entries. It was a joy reading and re-reading them and it will be a great pleasure to read them again.

My thanks to my fellow judges Joe Berger, Maia Bristol, Helen Hart and Tania Hershman for all the frank, honest and eye-opening discussions we had, proving that enjoyment of short stories is in the reading of them **and** discussions about them.

I would especially like to thank Joe Melia for his vision, passion, commitment and incredible organisational skills without which the Bristol Short Story Prize would be much the poorer. Also, the dedication of the readers for which we judges were incredibly grateful. Special thanks to Claire Shorrock for her wonderful cover design and to all the University of the West of England Illustration students who submitted designs and to course leaders Christine Hill and Jonathan Ward. Thank you to Arts Council England for their invaluable funding support. And, finally, a huge thank you to all the writers who sent in their stories.

One last thought; don't make reading short stories a private pleasure, share and discuss.

Bertel Martin
(Chair of 2011 Bristol Short Story Prize judging panel)

Judges' profiles

Maia Bristol

After many successful and creative years with Faber & Faber Maia recently left the company to pursue her freelance career in publishing and sales. She now lives happily with her husband and two young children in the picturesque village of St.Gilgen, just east of Salzburg. Maia also fits in library work with the local international school as well as developing her facility as a translator. Through all of these, she feels fortunate to see a huge variety of what the publishing world has to offer. But nothing, she believes, surpasses the variety in the entries for the Bristol Short Story Prize.

Joe Berger

Joe is a Bristol-based author, cartoonist, illustrator and animator. He has written and illustrated several picture books for Puffin, including *Bridget Fidget* and the sequel, *Bridget Fidget Hold on Tight!* He also co-writes and draws the *Pitchers*, a weekly 4 panel comic strip about screenwriters in the Guardian, and a single panel cartoon about food in the Guardian weekend magazine, both with his long-time collaborator Pascal Wyse. Joe and Pascal have created several award-winning animated shorts and a Bafta and Emmy nominated title sequence for the BBC drama *Hustle*. Joe lives in the Montpelier district of Bristol with his wife and their 3 daughters.

Tania Hershman

Passionate about short stories, Tania – whose first collection, *The White Road and Other Stories*, was commended in the *2009 Orange Award for New Writers* – founded *The Short Review* in 2007 to shine the spotlight on short story collections and their authors. Originally from London, Tania, a former science journalist, now lives in Bristol with her partner after spending 15 years in Israel. Tania is fiction-writer-in-residence at Bristol University's Science Faculty and is completing a collection of biology-inspired short fiction with funding from Arts Council England. Tania's award-winning stories and flash fiction have been published online and in print and broadcast on Radio 4. Tania's website is www.taniahershman.com and she blogs about writing at www.titaniawrites.blogspot.com and about being writer-in-residence at www.bris.ac.uk/science/blog.

Bertel Martin (Chair)

Bertel is a co-editor of *Bristol Review of Books* magazine and director of City Chameleon, a company that specialises in publising poetry and producing live literature performances. The process includes writer development and support, creating access to print for community groups and voluntary organisations and partnership working. Prior to setting up City Chameleon Bertel worked as a writer, performer, arts administrator and arts project manager in literature, dance, theatre in professional, community and education environments. He is also currently on the Board of Trustees for Circomedia, part of the steering group for the Sustained Theatre SW hub (to raise the profile of Black and Minority Ethnic theatre practitioners), www.citychameleon.co.uk

Helen Hart

Helen has been a published author since 1999. Represented by London literary agency Pollinger Ltd, she has written a number of novels under pseudonyms for Scholastic, Virgin Books and HarperCollins and has been a regular contributor to Emap Magazines' FHM. One of her Young Adult novels, written as Maya Snow, was shortlisted for the Solihull Children's Book Award 2010. As a co-director of Redwing Design, she supplies copywriting, editing and proofreading services for commercial clients. In 2007 Helen became the founding director of Bristol-based publisher SilverWood Books. www.silverwoodbooks.co.uk. She is the co-founder of the successful 'Get Published Masterclass' in Bristol (getpublishedmasterclass.wordpress.com). Helen lives in a small village south of Bristol with her husband and two teenaged daughters.

1ˢᵗ Prize
Emily Bullock

Emily Bullock graduated from King's College, London with an English degree and MA in 19th Century Literature. She followed this love of plot to work in feature film production before seeing the light and pursuing writing full-time. She attained a distinction from the UEA Creative Writing MA. Emily is currently tutoring for the Open University in Literature and Creative Writing and still writing, of course. She is, also, working on a Creative Writing PhD with the Open University.

My Girl

My job is to stop the blood, cool her off, wash her down. Who knows her better than her own mum? I rub the yellow car wash sponge across her head, smooth my fingers over the braids, sweeping away water with the back of my hand. Her coach leans over the ropes, whispering words I can't hear. All I have to do is make sure the match isn't stopped for bleeding. I open a jar and rub adrenalin chloride into the cut on her right cheek. Old scar tissue has ripped open, isn't much blood, but I'm not taking chances. My girl keeps her eyes on the other corner, but she lets me move her face from side to side, checking for fractures. Clean. An eyelash drops and curls onto my finger. I make a wish and send it on its way. The bucket of icy water has clouded pink but her reflection is steady. Nobody hears my wish.

Time is nearly up. I collect the bucket, towel and my toolbox of potions. I sit back down on the other side of the ring where it is darker, small pools of pale light collecting under the lamps on each table. I am one of them again: spectator. My girl stretches her arms and legs, letting the ropes take her weight, in the last seconds of rest. But the ring isn't empty. The men cheer as the bikini bulging girl, slipping in her white slingbacks, parades with the first round card held high above her yellow perm; howls loud as dogs left chained in a backyard, the air cold with moans.

I rub blue sanitizer into my hands. I don't want any dirt to get onto her broken skin. The liquid evaporates quick as tears; it smells as tart as the gin and tonics splashed across the tablecloths behind me. This is an exhibition fight, but the money is good and it will keep her in gloves and membership for six months. My girl watches it all. She shakes her head and water hits the floor in front of my shoes. The man behind me orders another round of whiskies and a cheer goes up.

The bell for the second round deadens the noise for a moment. My girl comes out tight, keeping hits away from the red lump swelling above her kidney. Her opponent is a swarmer. She comes at my girl again, happy to take hits on the ride in. Whisky splashes against my neck as a man behind waves his glass in the air. But my girl is fast. She blocks the blows without turning; eyes watching her opponent's muscles. Ready to knock and duck. Bang. My girl lands a punch to the side of the head. She circles and steps off again. Reach for it, reach for it, a man screams from behind his stack of pints; myopic eyes blinking through the glass.

No backdoor nightclub scratching and slapping here. Some cheer and some snigger behind napkins as they dab steak juice from their lips. Swift footwork smears blood into the canvas, pinned shadows which the fighters move around. A left upper cut to her opponent's chin silences the crowd. Splatters of red spin over the ropes and smack the front row; a spot balloons on my jeans. The other fighter's knees lock, a real pro and she stays standing. She pulls back, elbow in for power and slugs my girl deep in the gut. I can't breathe for her, can't feed her from my body anymore. Her eyes narrow and she circles; playing for time as she sucks down air to free the hot cramping pain. Her blue singlet and shorts turn black with sweat. After the fight, tonight, I will tell her. Enough. My girl took the punches even when she was a swollen bulge inside me.

It was a blow to the stomach finally woke me up. I was expecting it, my hands wrapped around her hidden body, leaving my head uncovered. He raised his foot above my face, but something stopped him: the banging from the neighbours upstairs, a siren on the street. He slammed the hallway door so hard it bounced right open again, did the same with the front door. I held on to the broken back of the chair, sat up and felt my girl kick. I laughed: all those doors wide open.

A draught from the fire exit blows litter in off the street, a crisp packet and burger wrapper circle and settle by the bucket. I boot them away. The cold air is no good for her muscles, but no one will hear me if I shout at them to close it again. The green light glows through the grey soup of smoke and beer belches. I shake the clean towels, plumping air into the folds.

They are locked together, tugging apart at the referee's shout. Her heart is fair beating out of her chest. She snorts air, nostrils flaring. But she isn't slowing. Her lip doesn't droop, her eyes aren't blinking. It is a good sign. Her coach signals with his hands, their secret language: a combination of hits or a change of tactics. She won't tell me their code. And that makes me proud. I'm here because she wants me. She's long past needing me to pull up her socks, wipe her nose, trim her crusts. So I wait for the bell to go, fold my bandages, mix my ointments to stop the cuts flowing. Hands working automatically as I watch her spin and circle around the ring. Her stretched plaits reveal the soft pink of her scalp; fontanelle toughened over the years, but I remember the first warm pulsing.

On the 18th December 1989, when waves smashed Blackpool pier and leaves whipped against windows, she began to fight. In the upstairs bathroom, on a blue fish and smiling dolphin beach towel, the ambulance delayed under a falling oak, my girl was born. She came out screaming: fists balled, face red, breathing hard. No one but me to hear her.

The bell goes for the third round. I am back at her side again. I squirt water into her mouth; collect it in the bucket as she spits it up. Wipe down her face and grease her skin to make the leather slide off. My nipples throb under the layers of jersey just like they did when she was a baby. I press a frozen eye iron to the top of her cheek, milking out the swelling. She lets me cradle her head, but tilts her ear towards the bell to better trap its sound.

She catches a couple of good hits in the third. One to the ribs. One to the back. A small cut is opening up under her right eye. It will need seeing to. She is hooking with her left and some of the men lean forward shouting encouragement, congratulating her coach. She's a born fighter, he tells them and waves his hand to show it is all he has to say.

I stood outside the gates on her first day of school, parents waving all around. And she asked me, what happened to my daddy? He was a fighter, I told her. If there were ever words I wish I could swallow back, they are it. The bruises he left me had long since yellowed and leaked away. She didn't ask anything else and I knew she'd get smart enough to fill in the rest. I watched her swing her orange PE bag over her shoulder and I waved until I thought my hands would drop off.

The fluorescent strip light coats her with its orange glue. With a right upper cut her opponent stuns her. I see her eyes as they flicker white. She glances over. All I can do is sit back and let it happen. The other fighter presses closer, forcing my girl's curling spine up against the ropes. Bang. Bang. Bang. A burst of hooks so fast, I'm not sure if I count three or four. But my girl won't go down. The light swings above the canvas, dividing up the ring, as they circle each other. Matched pound for pound, my girl stands an inch shorter than her opponent; but she meets her in the eye like they are the same height. No one has ever come close to knocking her down. Not that it stops me biting my lip and holding my breath.

When she was seventeen, out of school and out of work, she found her way to the gym. The boys there said, 'er's a funny 'un'. She didn't listen to them and went back every day it was open. She asked Bristol Pete, shoplifter to order, to fetch up some Everlast leather gloves, ten ouncers. I used to worry that she never came home until the sky outside the kitchen was one dark bruise, that welts and scrapes on her skin glowed red in the cold night air. I only let myself exhale when I heard her key in the lock. On Sundays she ran along the cold sucking sand, jumping dog shit the tide wasn't quick enough to wash away.

She swells in and out of the other fighter's reach, keeping in close and holding her guard up. My girl feints with a left and follows through with a smack from the right. She doesn't stay still to soak up the praise from the crowd. Feet seeming to float above the canvas as she pushes towards a neutral corner. My girl is punching smooth and fast, legs wide enough for balance but close enough that the petroleum jelly at the top of her thighs has rubbed off. Her skin will be turning red under those long silk shorts. My girl gets up close, ready to finish it. But her opponent isn't down yet; feet shuffling, shoulders dipping as she comes back at my girl. A deep blow under the belt, but they are too close, their bodies block the referee's view. Only I see it. That burning pain in her groin is spreading through her legs, slowing her down. She can't lower her hands, can't press the spot to deaden the pain. I crack an ice pack and get the water bucket ready. One sneaky left hook and bang, it could all be over for my girl too. Some punches in life you can't slip.

They're calling her The Blackpool Illuminator because she lights up the ring; that's what she told me over egg and chips, runny not set, a week before her first match. I knew why. It wasn't in her face, square and blunt like mine, or her hardened body. It was in the way she moved. Fork to mouth, knife to plate: stabbing out combinations, left and right. She pushed off from the balls of her feet as she got up to help me with the dirty plates. My girl balanced like a spinning top. I held my wrists under the cold water until I managed to squeeze out a smile for her.

The ice pack in my hand is numbing my skin. But I suck down hot air, whistling through my front teeth, as my girl takes a jab to the side of the face. Her head snaps back on her neck as the end bell goes. For one moment I taste the frozen silence of the hall, it fizzes and crackles on the heat of my tongue. But it isn't a sugared ice lolly taste. The points are totted up. The white shirted referee lifts an arm. Of course, the hometown fighter wins. Her fist smacks up into the air. The cheers aren't for my girl. Not this time. She slaps gloves with her opponent and crosses the canvas, back to me. But I keep my arms stiff at my side, so they can't open wide and pull her close.

Sweat runs into her eyes and she tries to flick at it with her gloves. I hold back her head and wipe her face dry with a fresh towel; press the ice pack to the base of her neck. I dab at the small cut under her eye, red and yellow, congealing already. Maybe if I hadn't wiped over her beginnings with that word, fighter, if she wasn't born in the great storm of '89, she wouldn't be up there now. But I can't imagine her any other way. Her opponent is carried off in a whirl of white teeth smiles and pumping arms. The audience is leaving, scraping chairs and slapping backs. I rub her down with the towels, cloak her body and legs. The men tug on jackets, sleeves turned inside out, fingers numbed by booze and legs deadened from steak and chips. 'I'll bring the car round,' her coach says as he gives her shoulder a pat.

A lone flash bulb bleaches her face. It's all done for the night. 'I lost,' she says. 'You didn't win this one but there'll be others,' I tell her. There won't be any story about my girl in The Echo, not tomorrow anyway. Search for her online and boxer puppies for sale from Blackpool kennels pops up. I hold open the ropes and she climbs out of the ring. She breathes in the coppery smack of blood, the taste of success. Together we walk through the blue ticket-stub and crumpled-napkin dust that the dinner jacket men have left behind. Sometimes we aren't the hero in our own stories: she fights and I stand in her corner, it's the way it will always be. Fists balled, face red. Breathing hard.

2ⁿᵈ Prize
Laura Windley

Laura Windley was born and brought up in Kent. She graduated from Sussex University with a degree in Psychology, then lived in various countries teaching English as a Foreign Language before returning to the UK and changing career. She now lives in sunny North London working as a production manager at a publishing house. In 2010 she had stories shortlisted and longlisted for the *Fish Publishing International Short Story Contest*. She writes whenever she can and *The Kitchen at the Lion* is her first published story.

The Kitchen at the Lion

'Freak', says the landlord of the Lion, gripping and flexing his hands on the bar. He glares as the door judders on its hinges and shuts with a dark clunk into the frame. A vein throbs in the damp pink of his temple and I can hear him breathing out from his nose. You can almost see the sweat seeping from the underarms of his nylon shirt, a vapour creeping up and around the men on their bar stools, infiltrating, in coils, the wood of the bar, the beer towels, the carpet.

The regulars sip from their tankards and lick the froth from their lips. The others, the joiners, I call them, dotted around, trying to hold their drinks as still as their breath. Beer dribbles down the side of pint glasses, dangles off bottom edges, quivers over the remains of others on sodden beermats.

The landlord only has to beckon with his head and the Fat Man waddles up and over to the door, wheezing with the effort. His belly dangles over his belt, as he reaches up and pulls the top bolt across, then down to the next and the next. The landlord snorts, starts wiping down the bar, muttering.

I set down my glass on my beer mat, calm as I can. I keep my eyes on the bar, don't look at the door. I feel one of the joiners looking over at me, slowly; me, with my hands on my jeans and my shirt sleeves up and bandana round my arm, just like one of them. Ordinarily, women aren't admitted – it's just Stella and me. None of the men look on us that way though – too old, too fat, too rough too fancy – but they do still need us, that's for sure. 'My girls,' the landlord calls us when he's in a good mood, 'my girls with their jobs to do.'

Down in the kitchen, Stella and I are beginning preparations for later. It'll be soup for the joiners and, depending on the meat, stew or pie for the regulars. Stella opens the plastic bag of meat on the worktop and sniffs. 'I don't know, Adele,' she says, screwing up her face, 'what d'you reckon?' I go over and take a look and it's not good. Dark grey-pink chunks. Juice looks watery. When I sniff, it catches at the back of my throat. 'Pie,' I tell her. 'With as much as we've got to hide the taste.' Stella nods and goes off to fetch her stash, her packets of spices. She keeps them hidden at the back of the cupboard, like treasure. I heat up the oil and hold my breath as I start frying the meat, dropping it in lump by lump, turning each one as it browns and the skin crisps, sizzling in the pan. There's sweat in my hairline and I can feel it starting to trickle down the back of my neck.

Stella has noticed that something's up today, even asks if I'm ok. She's sort of shy, though, she'd never push it if you said not to. I shrug and say 'Yeah?' and flash her the look that says 'Don't ask, mate' and although she frowns, she turns away. She's not a bad sort, not exactly a sparkler, but alright, for someone caught up with that lot upstairs. Lonely. So it's a pity, really. You can't let yourself get too caught up, but, y'know. I sigh and tell her I'm popping out for a smoke, can she get started on the soup and the veggies. 'Go on, then,' she says and smiles in a way that nearly breaks my heart, it's so trusting. It's like a puppy.

I go back up the stairs, past the edge of the bar. The regulars all sitting now, slurping, looking hollow-eyed, hollow-stomached up at the TVs in the corners. The TVs are covered in dusty fingermarks and they've got the blue scarves draped all over the tops. Underneath all the benches and chairs, in the corners, they've pushed their blankets and cushions, shoved in wherever they'll fit. Coats, too, stinky, from people sleeping under them. The cupboards upstairs are empty; people have to make do with the clothes they arrived in now, if he'll even let them in. They're all sat there now, waiting. No football to watch anymore, but old habits die hard.

The Fat Man reaches up and presses the on buttons, waddling importantly between the two as they flicker into life. The regulars and joiners all stare open-mouthed. It's just the one broadcast now, at five-thirty, from the network and the picture is always grainy. It's gone back to black and white and usually it crackles and you get a white line travelling down the screen like a wave. It can be hard to hear what they're saying, too. Sometimes they're in uniform and sometimes they're in suits, the men, but otherwise it's just like newsreaders in the old times. It lasts ten minutes, usually and tells you nothing but the same old same old. Prices up and down. Stocks running low. People in dots, masses of dots, black on the map, moving like swarms, from place to place, moving inland. I never bother to listen now, not really, it's like white noise. Just keeps them all quiet before they start getting drunk and lairy.

I push the door out to the beergarden and start searching. It's freezing, my hands are burning with cold as I light up my cigarette and I keep moving on the grass. It wouldn't be somewhere obvious, it just wouldn't. But it would be somewhere I know too, my boy's not stupid.. And it'll be small, I expect, not something you'd pick up on easily unless you were me. I try to remember, think, picturing him when he was small. Coming to places like this, in the summer, with us. He'd go off and try to find worms, he'd dig and crouch by the earth, watching. It's strange to imagine – such a big lad now. Taller than his dad ever was. When he was a kid, he'd be squeezed between us at the table, warm, folding empty crisp packets, seeing how small he could get them, squeezing them, smoothing them out, then licking the grease and salt from his fingers, concentrating, perfect alignment, folding in till they were smaller and smaller. And then he'd find them a slot. We used to laugh at him, the look on his face, frowning as he did it. You couldn't interrupt. And then he'd find a place for it, in a notch.

I go to the only table not rotten and sit myself one leg either side of the bench. My hands are red-raw with the cold now, swelling up. There's nothing obvious on top. I put the cigarette in my mouth and start feeling underneath the wood, gently, so as not to get splinters, finding the nicks. All the places between the table leg and the table, where the joins are. I try each one in turn until my fingers brush against something smooth. It's wedged in nicely, almost too nicely. He's forgotten I don't do fingernails. I scrape and pull, until it yanks down into my palm like a jewel. It's heavier than it should be, yes. This is it. I put my hand into the warmth of my pocket and squeeze my find between my thumb and finger, feeling the grains inside like sand. I don't dare look up or around, but I can sense it now. I stub my fag out on the hard earth and heave myself up.

I can feel the landlord staring the minute I get into the bar. I try not to look at him and walk on through but – 'Oi,' he yells, so the whole place reverberates. 'Yeah, you.' He beckons me over to the bar and I've got no choice, really, have I. 'What you been doing out there?' he says. My skin is beginning to prickle as the heat floods back into it. Out of the corner of my eye I can see Fat Man, crouched over one of the tables, looking up. I keep standing still, cross my arms, plant my feet into the carpet, so it feels like I'm pushing downwards, betraying nothing. I even raise my chin and make sure I breathe easy before I open my mouth. 'Smoking', I say. 'Getting some fresh air. It's hot down there, mate. I've got to have a breather sometimes.'

The vein pulses in his temple again, a worm, purple under his skin. He doesn't know what to say to me, his eyes bulge and the back of his jaw clenches. I remember once, men like this, this sort, standing in a crowd at a game. Shouting at the players on the field, their red faces, spit flying from their mouths and the way they'd turn on the crowd to gee them up. The look in their eyes. Screaming as hard at the people behind as at the team on the field, how once, I'd even put my hands over my kid's ears. Stella's talked about this too. 'Men are like dogs,' she told me once, 'always hunting in packs. But don't let them know I said it.' She's not all that stupid, really.

'That's rank,' he says finally. 'Not something I've ever had a taste for myself.' Cocks his head to the side, looks me up and down with contempt, like they always do to try to get the edge. I stand my ground and watch his nostrils flare. He snorts and turns back to the drinks. I reckon that's my cue to move off so I start walking backwards.

'Where did you say it was again, that old pub of yours?' he calls out behind him, pressing a double shot from a bottle. I watch as it squeezes out, honey into glass. My heart thuds in my ears like the sea. 'Brighton,' I say. 'Brighton,' he says, 'Right.'

When I get back down, Stella's got most of the job done. She's chopped all the veg and piled it up in a colander and there's onions frying, sauce bubbling, she's rolled out the pastry and lined the three dishes. Floury scraps are left all over the worktop, bits stuck to the rolling pin. She's standing there, sweating, wiping her hands on her jeans. 'You've been ages', she says, 'where you been?' 'Oh you know', I say, rolling my eyes. She nods. 'Right. Mind if I – .' 'No, no, mate, you go for it.' She heaves herself up the stairs, puffing up from the basement into the bar, her big arse wobbling as she climbs, a fag clutched backwards in her left palm.

I check the pans, pour the veg in, the stock, the barley. I learnt to cook from my grandma, back in the day and never have I been gladder of a skill; in fact, it's how I met Stella in the first place, years back and if it hadn't been for that – well. Chance is a funny thing. And there's the sauce bubbling and churning away, scum on the top of the simmering soup, steam rising.

I remember those days when my boy and the others were kids, all of them sitting and watching the sea. The tide coming in, land disappearing. Water lapping over the top of the old sunken pier, you could see more of it when the tide went out, the way the sun hit the water, blinding. I remember grains of salt in their hair. I'm not sure what happened to Stella's kids and I've never even asked, she never says, so I left it. Don't want to get too close. At the time, everyone said it couldn't happen, not long-term. But it did and I know everyone can't be trusted. The world has changed and that's the way it is. I reach inside my pocket and take out my treasure.

'Oi, Brighton.' The landlord's looming on the stairs. 'Get a move on will you.' I can see his shadow, its strange, square shape, clouding the white of the wall top to bottom. The stairs creak as he shifts his weight. 'Give us time. About another half an hour,' I shout up. Stella looks at me, flushed, her eyes full of warning. 'We don't have time,' he snarls. 'I've got them hungry up here.' 'We'll be there,' I say. 'We're going as fast as we can.'

He thuds down the stairs, pokes his head round the corner, glares at us. I glare back. 'What d'you want us to do?' I ask, opening the oven. 'Look.' The pies sit on their shelves, pale, ill-looking. 'Twenty minutes,' says Stella. He curls his lip. 'Fifteen.' I put my hands on my hips, take a deep breath. 'Fine,' I say. 'If that's what you want.' He nods. I look at my watch.

We take up the soups first. I ladle them out into bowls, send Stella up with the first two, steaming. I've put ours at the back of the cupboard, in the biggest bowl I could find, covered with a tea towel. It'll be cold but we can deal with that later and she'll be too busy to notice. I ladle out two more bowls and carry them up the stairs, hot liquid slopping over my thumbs and burning. The joiners' eyes are wild, their mouths slavering. Stella puts bread on the table and they tear into it, start slurping the soup down in gulps. In the background, the jukebox is playing some sad-sack music from the old days. We bring up the pies in their dishes, cut them up and serve in front of the rest, the landlord and the Fat Man first , of course; they lick their lips and the Fat Man's eyes are practically popping out of his head. He's squeezed in to one of the tables, his feet lifted off the floor and he even tucks a serviette into his collar. The landlord sits with him, at the head of the table. He doesn't take his eyes off me and Stella as he eats and I watch him shovelling it into his mouth, the sauce dribbling down his chin. Around is the clatter of knives and forks on plates, spoons on bowls, the sounds of them chomping, like animals, as we serve up the rest, every last one. Stella's in a rhythm, scooping, slopping, scooping, slopping, onto plates, until the dishes are empty and she's wiping her hands on her jeans and the sweat off her forehead.

Then we set to clearing the bowls and plates. The men are all sat, slumped, hands on bellies, satisfied, regulars and joiners alike. The landlord shoves his plate across the table and sits back in his chair, lets out an exaggerated sigh. God, I hate him, sat there, with his fingers clasped together, his red face, his white hair, white eyebrows, the muscles in his neck. My stomach is in a hard knot, rising. The back of my neck is starting to bristle and I'm hoping I'm not imagining the subtle change in the air. I can feel it, now, almost smell it in the air, that he is nearby, with the rest. I can't stay up here, just can't. I gather a pile of plates and trying to stop my knees wobbling, make my way down the stairs, my arms heavy. Down in the basement, I close my eyes for a second and pray and imagine it, get the feel of it, like the cloud rolling in, or the waves, getting closer and closer. I start to wash up, it's the only thing I can do, with the feeling in my stomach rising up and up, pushing the breath out in short, sharp bursts, my throat tightening my jaw. I keep focused, focused on the suds and the rhythm of me scrubbing, my hands warm in the water, willing and afraid. It won't be long till all of them are gone; lolling on the tables, falling to the floor. Come on, come on. Where are you all?

There's crashing and a clatter from upstairs, an almighty thud. Groans. Smashing glass. Slurring and yelling like any night but all at once. And then Stella thundering heavy down the stairs, her face contorted, her eyes wide, in panic. 'Adele, there's people outside,' she says. 'A big crowd of them.' I look up at her, say nothing. Everything drops from me suddenly, like my skin falling off and piling at my feet. The world changes. The particles in the air realign, the colours shift. I step out of my old skin and forward. My son is there and that's all that matters. My boy. My heart is thick in my throat. I wipe my hands.

'Oh my god, what have you done?' she gasps, 'Adele. What have you done?' I have never seen her so alive. I climb up the bottom stairs and face her, grip the top of her arms. Look straight at her. Every line, every pore of her sagging skin. Like mine, like looking into a mirror. Her eyes, blue, searching for answers. 'Are they passing out, has it worked?' I ask and her mouth opens, wordless and her eyes brim with saltwater. Mine are beginning to sting. I hold my arm out to her with the blue bandana and watch as with trembling hands, Stella begins to unpick the knot.

3ʳᵈ Prize
Laura Lewis

Laura Lewis migrated as a child from maple tree country to an olive tree zone. There's been nursing school, mandatory military service, art school, cleaning jobs, teaching and a bakery to contend with ever since. Her second migration was to the land of the healing tea tree where she lives happily with her husband in New Zealand, though markets with spices in conical spheres still have their allure. A very good day is spent ironing the crumple out of words. On a perfect day, she knows what to do with them. *Reading Turkish Coffee* is her first published work.

Reading Turkish Coffee

Alma's slowing down. Only her broom seems to keep her from landing in a heap on the ground. Her garment looks heavier than she is. Layers of cloth are divided by flattened rope; the hem brushes her ankles. Whether the garment is gown, dress or robe is unclear.

Art students surround her, hungry to prove how original they are: as she mops her way through the school, eyes glued to the ground, she alone is unique.

Over the weekend there was a party and Alma's filled more plastic bags than a checkout girl. Fuchsia, pink and plain tipped butts, smoked to the filter or discarded midway fill the bags. A student approaches, sees treasures in the bags. 'It will make a great collage,' she says. 'If she were my daughter,' Alma thinks, 'I'd cut off financial support.' It's meaningless, though: she's invisible to this young woman.

Avi calls her for their morning break. He's making Turkish coffee: three times the coffee and water are heated just to the boil and cooled. 'Last round.' He tips the pot by its handle and pours. They're both looking tired and the week's just begun. As they sit, there's a knock at the door. 'Can you give me a reading today?' Sarita is in her final year at the academy. Her parents, like Alma, come from Syria. She makes Alma laugh, using expressions in broken Arabic and getting them wrong.

'Tomorrow. Your party made extra work.'

'I have a friend, he could use some direction.'

'Bring him along. Shut the door on your way out, be a good girl. The heat is escaping.'

The one rung heater allocated to maintenance staff wouldn't warm a guppy. Alma shivers and pulls her robe close. She washes them daily and by alternating two sets she usually has dry clothes for work but today they're damp and she's feeling under the weather. Avi turns the heater in her direction with his foot.

Alma holds the cup with ladylike breeding and sips. When it's empty, she places a saucer over the top and turns it upside down. Handing it to Avi, she says, deadpan,

'I could use some direction.'

He lets the sediment dry; the coffee grinds cake the sides with symbols and omens.

Avi and Alma are makeshift family, working together for the better part of the past decade. His family attended her son Sam's graduation from law school: the happiest day of her life. She was given a place of honour at his daughter's wedding.

She knows he doesn't like reading for her: she taught him the art but next to her he's an amateur. Alma reads the grinds to uncover the truth; she's rather spectacular at it, like a courtroom lawyer. Though Avi has learned to recognize the symbols, he falters trying to give context to what he sees.

'Wouldn't it be easier just to tell me what's on your mind?' he says.

'No.' She doesn't like wasting words.

His eyebrows bump like magnets. He lifts his eyes and she sees that he's worried.

'It's alright,' Alma says 'I've already read it myself.'

'You can't read your own future.'

'I was bored.'

'Are you playing cat and mouse with me?'

Alma doesn't answer or smile. She reaches for her broom but Avi stops her. 'Don't go. I'll tell you what's here. I see a mask, something hidden. I see a door.'

Student activity past their little room is slowing down. The break must be over. Avi hesitates as Alma waits, a detached look on her face. 'Is a ghost bothering you?'

'No one's bothering me.'

'Good.'

'As long as he keeps his hands off of Sam I've got no problem with him.'

'So the ghost is a he?'

Alma turns her back and walks off.

The No. 8 bus is crowded in summer, even more so in winter when overcoats and boots suck up the last of the empty space. Alma pushes past younger passengers and claims a seat as it's being vacated. She balances a kilo bag of clementines between her feet and starts to drift. She saw the same things that Avi saw in her coffee. Ghosts are real but she doesn't believe one is haunting her now. You don't need a ghost to explain all that's wrong. A real husband can haunt, she figures, even after twenty five years. He'll still be alive if she knows the old coot.

Down King George Street the bus pulls in and out of traffic and daylight fades. As it passes King Solomon Road, rain taps the windowpanes, in front of King David's Luxury Hotel the street lights turn on like a well practiced cue. The familiar route lures her to sleep.

A boy with dark hairs on the back of his fingers is patting her hand. She wakes with a start. The bus is almost empty now; it must be near her stop at the end of the line. The boy is handing her the bag of clementines. His eyes are honey brown and almond shaped and for the life of him he looks like Sam did at that age.

'The bag spilled, but I think they're all here.'

'God bless you,' she says automatically, in spite of long since having broken with God. Then adds, 'You're a good boy.' She sees he's embarrassed and smiles at him. 'You'll make your mother proud,' she says, but softer, not for him to hear but as a blessing.

She's first at work the next day. All the doors are unlocked, lights turned on and rubbish collected by the time the secretary waltzes in.

She murmurs 'hello' at the spot above Alma's head. Alma pretends not to see her so she needn't respond. It's a ritual. The head of the department enters, 'Good morning, Alma,' he says brightly, too much emphasis on being the good guy for her taste.

The weekend arrives. Her son and his fiancée visit. Now she's Mamma, flashing a wide smile, gold front tooth exposed and glinting.

Throughout lunch, Ruby nibbles like a little mouse on bits of lettuce and carrots that garnish the dishes Alma spent hours preparing. After lunch, she insists Ruby and Sam sit on the sofa, pulling an ottoman close for herself. Ruby's in the kitchen now, making tea. She drinks her coffee as well as tea black, because she wants to fit in a wedding dress two sizes too small.

'I think she's already a very good size,' Alma says when Ruby's out of the room.

'It's a matter of what's fashionable, Mamma, times have changed.'

'Well, thank God for that,' she thinks, 'one way to be a few sizes smaller when you're a bride is to be married off when you're twelve. Thank God indeed times have changed.'

'Mamma, when are you going to retire?' He's asked her before. She hates it, thinks it's bullying.

'When I'm dead.' Ruby comes in with the tea.

Alma stands up: I'm going to pick some mint.' The garden's out back, near the gas balloons and stray cats. She takes her time, breathing the fresh air, aware that it's free and undeniably wonderful.

She knows it galls Sam that she won't accept help. He has a proper shot at life now and she wants him to grab it with both hands. There weren't other offspring of cleaning ladies in his class at law school. Maybe he's ashamed, maybe just worried for her. In any case, she's not giving up work. Back inside, she asks 'Have you set a date for the wedding yet?'

'We're hoping for May. We're still trying to book a venue.'

'I hope you're not waiting in case your father shows up.'

Sam and Ruby exchange a married couple's kind of glance. 'What a thing to say, mamma,' he says with distaste.

Alma turns evasive, like she behaves when at work. Blank, she nibbles cinnamon bark and refuses to talk.

Not many days elapse before the phone rings. Wires cross live under the city; somebody hangs up before she finds out who it is. Half an hour later, the phone rings again. 'Do you recognize my voice?' a man says.

'Why do you call? I don't need a ghost in my life.'

'But I'm very much alive,' he insists.

What are the odds, she wonders. Then the line goes dead, leaden silence replaces the wispy voice. Alma pulls the phone from the jack in the wall. She prepares a cup of tea and sets a few cushions on the edge of the sofa. After all of these years she doesn't need that ghost popping up. Superstition and old age are settling into her middle aged bones.

She falls asleep on the sofa, before the sun sets, before dinner. Instead of hugging a hot water bottle in bed, her legs protrude stiffly through the space formed by the wooden armrest. She dreams she's a wolf corpse strung on a hunter's stick, then wakes when night mingles with day's first nudge. She hopes the phone call was only a dream.

The phone rings again the next evening. His voice says 'Don't hang up Alma.'

There was a place she called home a long time ago, close to where Syria and Turkey meet like waves lapping sand. Aleppo, the silk route city. Her first memory is colourful scarves. Magenta and turquoise and gold. Navy and crimson and daffodil. Colours soft, colours pungent, bright, aching. Smelling of overripe fruit and new leaves.

Her father kept a globe on his desk and she spent hours tracing countries with her finger, learning names of places she could only dream of. She wondered if the earth changed colours like they did on the globe.

From her window one day she saw a man cross the courtyard. She had been to his house with her mother and father, when all were invited to partake of refreshments after the synagogue service. She assumed he had business with her father. She wandered into the garden in the back courtyard. Her mother ambushed her there, carrying a tray. Slices of earth coloured candied quince on blue and white china, passion fruit rolled unadorned in a chesty glazed bowl. There was a sharp, pearl handled knife, two silver spoons and two forks.

'Bring these to your father and his guest. Keep your eyes down.' She smoothed her daughter's braid. 'Knock before you enter father's study. Don't spin the globe. That will look like you want to stay, understand?'

Alma knew she was in danger of laughing out loud. 'Why would I want to stay in the room with some old man?'

'Don't talk like that, it will bring you bad luck,' her mother said.

'Alma, light of my eyes,' her father said one day soon after, when she had turned twelve. 'It is time for you to get married. I have arranged a marriage to a good man, one who will make you comfortable.'

'I don't want to get married yet,' she told him

'It is for your own good.'

'I still want to live here, with you and mamma.'

'Yet this marriage is in your best interest, you'll see. You are young and strong, but no beauty. This man has a good heart. His other wife will be like a mother to you. You will like his children.'

Nobody was home. Her older sister was already married. Her mother had gone to see her new grandchild. Her father was away on business, old Miriam was preparing the midday meal. Alma knocked on her parent's bedroom door, just in case, then turned the door handle. She sat down in front of her mother's vanity set, taking care not to disturb the pots with colours and crèmes, the sticks for kohl and miniature brushes. She looked at herself as though the mirror had just been invented. The outer edges of her eyelids drooped, giving her a mournful appearance. Her eyelashes were skimpy. Her father was right, she's no beauty. In any case, girls her age became brides. She decided not to fuss.

So they dressed her in bright clothes, strung coins from her forehead, poked holes in her ears and she became a second wife, joining a household with children not much younger than herself. Her son was born on her fourteenth birthday and she saw it as an omen of good things to come. But those good things had to wait until a wave of pogroms ended, restoring safety to everyday life. By the time Sam was running on his toddlers' ridiculously optimistic legs, hope was abandoned. There was a journey to the Syrian border at midnight; a household reduced to a single filed row, one husband, one middle aged wife, one child bride, a toddler with cherry lips and old eyes, the middle-aged man's offspring from the first wife and a bagful of 'baksheesh' – kickback money to buy their way out of Syria and pave a new life in the promised land.

The guards liked the colour of money. They said: 'everybody crosses the border but you, old man. We are turning you back.' And so it was. The middle-aged wife, her children and the teenage mother of one crossed the border and the old man went home, penniless. With no one to remind him who he is, he might as well have been a ghost.

In the Promised Land they were sent to a city of tents. In time, the government turned the tents into matchstick houses, ugly, utilitarian, subsidized. In summer, the colour palette is blue sky and yellow sun, colours flat and plain as a beach ball. People in this development are good for cooking or cleaning or factory work. Alma laughs to herself: does anybody need a dreamer of colours and tracer of countries? She accepted a cleaning job at an art school, thinking 'this is where my luck would have me.'

Back at work Avi is whitewashing walls and Alma spreads newspaper on the floors. Sarita's friend, the one whose fortune she read the previous week, approaches her.

'Did Sarita tell you things about me?' He is agitated, inhaling a cigarette like he wants to smoke two for the price of one. 'I mean, could you really just have 'seen' the things that you said?'

Alma doesn't have time for him.

'Why are you walking away?'

Alma sits on her haunches against a wet wall before Avi can stop her. Her robe covers her lower body like a blanket.

She covers her face, as if to escape: away from this young man who still thinks like a boy. Away from art students who cannot see, as she does, in colour. And far away from the old man who she knows is now near.

'Because I don't like you, that's why.'

Later that day she gets off at the last stop. She heads down an alley, shoos a dog from her path, puts her bags down to unlatch the gate. An old man is leaning against the wall. 'Are you lost?' Alma says, not wanting to look at him. She fumbles with her key ring: in her agitation, she can't find the right one.

'Not anymore,' he says. They both look down, minutes pass.

Alma says 'Well, come in then.'

His eyes latch onto her as she carries out her end of the day routine. The years have played tricks, in his absence their age gap has narrowed. When they went to the border she was almost sixteen and he was well over double her age. She's now forty-six, looks years older and he is just sixty-six, or would that be seventy? With some luck, he could outlive her. It could go either way.

He tells her of people who stayed back. Then he pulls a shimmering scarf from his bag like a magician and another and another again. As he hands them to her, she doesn't look down fast enough. His eyes: they're nice, like Sam's eyes. She never noticed before.

Out back, picking mint for their tea, she breathes the chilly night air and feels her lungs expand: alive, still alive, for now, for tonight. It was nice making dinner for two.

She's rethinking the way that she looked at the grinds: there's been some powerful luck which has kept him alive.

Ruth Brandt

Ruth Brandt hasn't stopped writing since she half-heartedly signed up for a creative writing evening class 12 years ago and became inspired. She has recently had short stories published in *Litro* magazine both online and print. Her work has also appeared in a *Leaf Books* anthology, *Yours* and *Candis* magazines, competition anthologies and online. She teaches Creative Writing at Surrey ACL and has a degree in Maths and Physics. Born and raised in Bristol, Ruth now lives in Surrey with her two sons and is currently working on a novel.

'No one has any intention of building a wall'

(Walter Ulbricht, Head of the German Democratic Republic (DDR), 14th June 1961)

It's 5.30 p.m. on Saturday 12th August 1961 and Gabi Liebknecht is standing outside her grandmother's apartment in Bernauer Strasse, Berlin, leaning her back against the pockmarked wall. Casually she glances at the house opposite where Peter lives. Peter is fifteen and has blonde hair and blue eyes and two days ago he stopped to ask her name. She hasn't seen him since and now she thinks he must be out.

Click, clack, round the corner come two French soldiers, guns over their shoulders, click, clack, click, clack. Gabi rests a foot behind her on the wall. One of the soldiers slows as he approaches.

'Gabi,' her grandmother calls down from the window. 'Come in and help.'

The soldier smiles down at Gabi and says something. Gabi doesn't speak French.

'Now, Gabi.'

'Coming, Oma,' Gabi calls.

The soldier repeats what he's said, all the words running into one like a waterfall. She smiles back.

'Now, Gabi,' Gabi mimics.

The soldier laughs and rests his hand briefly on her shoulder, before striding off to catch up with his colleague. She watches the pair turn into Ruppiner Strasse, the heat of his palm still on her skin.

Gabi is fourteen, too old to be sent to stay with her grandmother while her parents visit her father's aunt in Hanover, but she knows she isn't here for her own sake. Oma is lonely, her mother says and her memory isn't what it used to be; and then there's her hip; and anyway, Gabi has always spent time here during the summer holidays when the rest of her friends head off to the lake at Wannsee, or across to West Germany to visit relatives. Why change now?

Running her fingers over the bullet holes, Gabi saunters to the door of 48 Bernauer Strasse and as she steps from the pavement into the lobby, she leaves the French sector of Berlin and enters the Soviet sector. Sixteen years ago someone, somewhere had decreed that the front wall of Gabi's grandmother's block of apartments should constitute the boundary between the two zones, leaving the inhabitants living in East Berlin, but their only entrance and exit in the west.

'Guten Tag.' Ida Siekmann's door on the first floor shoots open, as though she has been waiting all afternoon to hear footsteps. 'Are you staying with your grandmother again?'

'Yes, Frau Siekmann,' Gabi replies. 'Just for two weeks.' Then she adds, 'Mutti and Vati are in Hanover.'

'Hanover.' Ida Seikmann nods her head.

Frau Seikmann hasn't been here long. She moved from Gorki, Poland, to be near her sister a couple of blocks away in French administered Wedding. Oma repeats this news to Gabi often, except Oma still calls Gorki Gorken and says it's in West Prussia.

'Why do they have to mess around with countries?' Oma says a lot. Gabi has given up commenting.

Having repeated 'Hanover', Frau Siekmann waits. She has no one other than her sister, Oma says, not since the war and never anything to say.

Inside the Siekmann apartment Gabi spies a hat on a chair and the plastic handbag that all women in East Berlin carry, marking them out when they come over to the west of the city. And she has the same cream sofa and wooden table and cream TV that everyone in East Germany – the DDR – has, not Oma though who still has her furniture from before the war.

'How's school?' Ida Siekmann asks.

Gabi watches the wrinkles in Frau Siekmann's face open and close as she speaks and she wonders how old she is. Sixty perhaps. Gabi doesn't know.

'Good, thank you,' Gabi answers. 'It's the holiday now.'

'Ah, yes.'

Frau Siekmann's hand fiddles with her door latch.

'Oma was calling me.'

As though relieved that an end to the conversation has been found, Frau Siekmann steps back inside her flat.

'You'd better go,' she says.

'Good evening, Frau Siekmann.' Gabi waves as she runs on up the stairs.

In the kitchen, Frau Schmidt, from the ground floor, is sitting at the table. Oma is shaking her head as a pan of potatoes bubbles away.

'Frau Schmidt has come to tell us that Doctor Brecht has left,' she says.

Frau Schmidt talks to Oma like this all the time now; the dentist has left, fields of corn out in the countryside lie unharvested because the farmers have left, there's no one to teach the children; everyone is leaving the DDR for the West. Frau Schmidt's world is full of this talk.

'Who's going to look after my Hans now?' Frau Schmidt adds.

Hans Schmidt was only four years old when he was shot in the face by the advancing Soviet troops in May '45. He has one eye and repeated infections in the remaining empty socket.

'They won't leave us with no one,' Oma says. She believes this.

'Twelve and a half thousand East Germans have left for the west this week alone,' Frau Schmidt says.

The borders that stem the flow of emigrants between East and West Germany elsewhere don't work in Berlin where Berliners, East and West, criss-cross the city every day for work. Berlin is a loophole where East Germans can travel to make day visits to relatives in West Berlin, carrying only a small bag of belongings to show they have every intention of returning home. And with that small bag they start their new lives in the West. Vast transit camps have been set up in West Berlin to gather together the skilled and educated emigrants. And all this is possible because the victorious Second World War allies divided the country's capital city, now located deep within the DDR, into four, in preference to letting it fall into the hands of the Soviets.

'He could see Doctor Litfin.' Gabi suggests her own family doctor in an attempt to stall Frau Schmidt's gathering rant.

'He could see Doctor Litfin,' Oma repeats.

'If we can travel down to Kreuzberg,' Frau Schmidt replies.

Gabi stabs a potato to see if it's cooked. It's this sort of talk that really irritates Gabi now she's fourteen and knows a bit about the world. Who's going to stop Frau Schmidt taking the one-eyed Hans to see Doctor Litfin five kilometres away in American administered Kreuzberg?

'I hear that today border guards are stopping trains coming into Berlin and interrogating passengers.' Frau Schmidt shakes her head. 'Most are being sent back to where they came from.'

'No one will stop us travelling around in Berlin,' Gabi says, banging the pan in the sink as she drains the water. 'The Americans won't allow it.'

The Americans, British and French didn't let the Soviets starve them out in 1948 and they maintain secure transport links between West Berlin and the rest of West Germany. The Americans will look after them. Oma nods.

'Maybe the Americans don't care about us anymore.' Frau Schmidt crosses her arms.

'Doctor Litfin might travel here to see Doctor Brecht's patients,' Gabi says, steering the conversation away from Frau Schmidt's speculation.

'A doctor visit Soviet Berlin when he's free!' Frau Schmidt laughs.

'They won't leave us without doctors,' Oma says.

Gabi sets out the knives and forks for the evening meal, brushing against Frau Schmidt's arm to show her she's in the way. Frau Schmidt takes the hint.

'I better get back to my Hans,' she says.

Only once she's gone, does Gabi ask:

'Will Mutti and Vati be all right getting back from Hanover?'

'Why couldn't those people leave our country as it was?' Oma replies and Gabi wishes she hadn't said anything.

As Gabi piles potatoes onto the plates, Oma puts an arm round her waist and for a brief moment Gabi lets her cheek rest on her grandmother's crinkly hair. But the hair prickles and she pulls away to add a wurst to each of the plates.

Later, in her bedroom, Gabi rubs her soap-dry hands and looks down into hot Bernauer Strasse, hoping to catch sight of Peter. She can't wait to get back home and tell her friends about him. She's not tired and yet it's bedtime, so she lies down on top of her eiderdown and splays her hair out over the pillow to cool. Dull, dull, dull. She counts the remaining days.

Gabi thinks she must have overslept for all the commotion going on outside in the street; talking, shouting, running. The curtains are glowing dim and it feels far too early for such movement. And then she remembers it's Sunday in any case. From the kitchen she hears Frau Schmidt's voice. She steps out of bed.

'Is that a risk you're prepared to take?' Frau Schmidt is saying.

They are drinking coffee, Frau Schmidt and Oma, in Oma's kitchen. Gabi rubs her face; can it really be late enough for Frau Schmidt to be visiting?

'What's the time?' she asks, blinking the blur from her eyes.

'I'm staying put.' Oma tops up the coffee.

Gabi focuses on the clock. It's five past seven. There's a rap at the door, sharp enough to make the women start.

'Shall I open the door?' Gabi asks.

'More fool you,' Frau Schmidt says.

At the door stands Hans, his one eye staring at Gabi. Gabi has never liked Hans; he has always known what he wanted and, because of his one eye, has always been given it. Last year, in the stairwell, he shoved her into the corner, his hot body heavy against hers and he had grabbed at her breasts, put his hand up her skirt, rooted around until she had wriggled a hand free and poked him in that empty eye socket, made it bleed, reawakened a latent infection. This year she stands well back to let him pass. He doesn't dawdle.

'I've been all the way up Schwedter Strasse,' he reports. 'And along Garten Strasse. There's barbed wire and border guards everywhere. All crossings are closed. The Brandenburg Gate is closed. Everyone's saying the barbed wire is temporary,' he pauses. 'They're going to build a wall.'

'Oh my god, it's true!' Frau Schmidt shrieks and grabs her one-eyed son. 'Thank God you're safe.'

'The Westies are gathering on the other side, shouting at the guards,' Hans continues.

'The Westies!' Oma claps her hand down on the table. 'There are no Westies or Easties; we are all Berliners. This city cannot be divided by barbed wire or a wall or anything. The Americans will not allow it.'

'Just look out at the street, Oma,' Hans says, hands in pockets, his good eye rolling up in its socket. Gabi wants to shove her sharp nails into that empty space all over again.

'We're going home to pack,' Frau Schmidt says.

'It'll be back to normal tomorrow,' Oma says.

'You're deluded,' Frau Schmidt says.

And Frau Schmidt and Hans are off, down the stairs, into their apartment to pack a suitcase or two, before stepping out of 48 Bernauer Strasse onto the free, French pavement in West Berlin while their front door still allows.

'Shall we go, Oma?' Gabi asks.

'Your mother was born in this apartment,' Oma replies. 'And here,' she pats the table, 'this is where I heard the news that your Opa had been crushed to death in Luisen Strasse, searching for food for his family while those bastards bombed the life out of us.'

'What if Frau Schmidt's right?'

'Your parents will be back next week,' Oma says. 'Then you will go home.'

It's early morning on Tuesday 22nd August 1961 and Gabi Liebknecht's grandmother is still asleep. Nothing more has been heard from Frau Schmidt and Hans, or the fifty other households in Bernauer Strasse who took the opportunity to flee. A number of East German border guards, one of whom features prominently in foreign newspapers, jumping with his rifle over coiled barbed wire, have also escaped. The U-bahn trains, which 10 days earlier linked West to East to West, no longer stop at Bernauer Strasse underground station, or any other station in East Berlin. Instead they clatter through the dimly lit, well-guarded, ghost stations on their route between the French north and American south. The flow of Germans from the DDR has slowed from a deluge to a faltering trickle, just like that, overnight.

Over the past four days the East German authorities have been making slow progress up Bernauer Strasse, bricking in the doors and windows on the south side of the street which once gave direct access to the west. Today, they have arrived at 48 Bernauer Strasse with their bricks and mortar. Already there is no front door; the exit to the building is now a temporary opening bashed in at the back, securely located in the Soviet administered sector.

Until today, Gabi's grandmother has stood firm. They have heard nothing from Gabi's parents and have no idea whether they have been able to return from Hanover, so Gabi has remained. In any case, if there really is to be no possibility of travel between the two halves of the city, who will look after the old, failing woman if Gabi goes?

Looking out at the houses on the north of Bernauer Strasse, Gabi sees Peter leaving his front door, off to meet up with friends, perhaps, or to listen to Elvis. She waves at him and he hesitates before crossing the street. She opens the window.

'Why are you still there?' he calls up to her.

'I'm taking care of Oma,' she replies and to her, her words, called down to the blonde haired Peter, sound not just practical but romantic.

'You are mad to stay so long. You must leave, today. Look!'

Gabi knows that the bottom floor of their building is already bricked up and that the guards are now moving up to Frau Siekmann's apartment on the first floor.

'I will talk to Oma,' she says.

'Don't talk,' Peter replies. 'Tell her.'

Gabi smiles and nods and then Peter does something which angers her.

'You're bloody stupid,' he shouts and as he turns away the ridiculousness of her romantic notions hit her.

Without waking her grandmother, she packs her few things. All is not yet lost; each day so far the West Berlin fire brigade have been in Bernauer Strasse, holding out jumping sheets for people escaping from higher rooms. There is no longer any doubt in her mind that she will be waiting for them when they turn up shortly, as they surely will.

There's a knock at the front door. Gabi hesitates, fearing that the guards have already come to move them away from the apartment further into Soviet territory. She curses herself for her idiocy in staying so long.

'It's Frau Siekmann,' a woman's voice whispers. 'Ida.'

For a moment Gabi isn't sure. Perhaps Frau Siekmann has been put up to this by the guards to trick Gabi into opening.

'Please let me in,' Frau Siekmann says.

Gabi opens the door a crack, peers through it at the landing and, seeing only Frau Siekmann, lets her slip in.

'They are in my apartment,' Ida Siekmann tells the 14-year-old.

Gabi's heart pounds, her throat tightens.

'The fire brigade will be here shortly,'she says. 'We'll jump.'

Frau Siekmann passes her plastic handbag from one hand to the other; a very small bag, the one she would have carried with her on a visit to her sister's two weeks ago, nothing much in it at all. Her eyes dart, her mouth opens and closes, taking tiny little clips of air.

'I must go to my sister,' she says.

From downstairs Gabi hears guards' boots pounding.

'In the front,' she says, pointing to her room while she hurries to deal with her grandmother.

The news later that day, reported by the international press gathered in Bernauer Strasse, tells of Ida Siekmann dropping an eiderdown onto the pavement, followed by a few possessions and then, before the firemen were able to open their jumping sheet, she threw herself out. Nothing much is known about her, except that now Ida Siekmann, who died on her way to the hospital, is the first casualty of the wall.

Back up on the second floor, Gabi first hears yells from the street. She looks out and recognises the flowers on her eiderdown. Her grandmother stirs. Gabi looks from Oma to the small ring of people fussing over a pile of clothes down below. She is fourteen with strong bones and a strong mind. Oma has neither. Downstairs boots crunch and trowels scrape cement. She waves at the firemen.

'Here,' she calls. 'Here.'

And as they gather beneath her grandmother's bedroom window, Gabi grabs a photo of Oma, Opa and Mutti. She grabs her grandmother's comb, because it comes readily to hand and a cushion that Mutti embroidered as a child.

'Oma,' she says, shaking the precious woman awake. 'We're leaving.'

'I'm not ...'

'Now,' Gabi says and she throws the handful of her grandmother's belongings down onto the jumping sheet, followed by her own small case. 'It's not hard. See.'

Her grandmother shakes her head. Gabi leads her to the window.

'You go first, Oma. I'll follow.'

'I'm not leaving.'

'You must.' Gabi blinks and swallows. 'There's no life for us two here. We need to be with Mutti and Vati. They'll look after us. We can't be here alone.'

And as she sits on the window ledge, legs dangling outside, words of encouragement are shouted up from the street.

'Take my hand, Oma. Sit with me, here. Just sit. That's it. Now swing your legs round. Please, Oma. There, that's it. Hear what they're saying? Push outwards, shuffle your bottom forward and push off outwards. Hear them, Oma? Please don't cry. We'll be OK.' Gabi smiles. 'There,' she says, pointing. 'See, it's Mutti. She's waving at us. We must go to her, Oma. Do it now, I'll follow. Everything will be all right.'

Timothy Bunting

Timothy Bunting is a Journalism graduate from Australia, currently living in London. He has worked in a variety of odd jobs (odd being the operative word) and writes in his spare time. There is a novel somewhere in his head and he is planning to complete a MA in Creative Writing upon his return to Australia to help it come out.

Himitsu-Bako

A hundred female faces look at him from the screen. All cropped according to the site's requirements, they seem identical at first glance. Stephen scrolls down the screen until one face sticks out.

Stephen finally opts for a pair of polished leather brogues with a slight heel. They have small pieces of metal in the sole which make a noise on a hard surface. He imagines this will confer some level of confidence, perhaps even status, so he feels they're a suitable choice. And he's vain and nervous enough to need them tonight.

When she finally arrives at the restaurant (carpeted, typically), some twenty-five minutes after the agreed time, Stephen is hunched at the bar wearing a helpless expression. If she had come on time, she would've seen him sitting with an appropriated masculine posture (straight-backed, shoulders relaxed – a stoic attempt), with a gin and tonic (less oafish than a pint, but not too effeminate).

She's wearing a sleeveless scarlet dress, tight, but not suffocating and her lithe arms grip an impractically bulky handbag. Her black stockinged legs perch upon vertiginous stilettos. She is subtly made up and her accessories are modest, although her lips wear a thick layer of red lipstick. As she approaches he straightens up and greets her effusively.

'Red goes faster,' she says ironically, by way of greeting.

Dinner is cordial, restrained. Both parties are inexperienced and tentative and it's only towards the end of the meal, lubricated by several glasses of wine that they begin to feel comfortable.

'You've got sauce on your shirt,' says Erika, smiling.

Stephen looks down and notices a spot of balsamic jus halfway down his chest. He tries to wipe it off with his napkin but only lengthens the smear.

Erika's apartment is something like a minimalist art exhibit. The living room is bare besides a plush grey sofa. No television, bookcase, decorations. Bright white walls, hardwood floor. Stephen's shoes make a satisfying clunk as he steps inside.

'How do you like your coffee?' she asks.

'Black, thank you.'

The kitchen, tidy, chrome, angular. Like a showroom.

'You own this place? says Stephen.

'It's my parents' place. They recently moved back to Japan.'

'Were you born in Japan?'

'In Hakone, not far from Tokyo. My parents moved to London when I was one.'

'That explains your accent.'

'What's wrong with my accent?'

'Nothing. It's just very...refined.'

'Well, I am Japanese.'

Erika's bedroom is contrary to the rest of the apartment. Shelves stacked with books, photos, small mementoes. One shelf holds an array of puzzles; a Rubik's cube, a couple of warped bits of metal, some wooden games, a Tower of Hanoi. A huge mahogany bed dominates the room.

'Did you know there are over forty quintillion permutations in a Rubik's cube?' she asks.

'I've never even heard of that number.'

'Are you good at puzzles?'

'Not really.'

Erika reaches up to the shelf and takes down what Stephen originally thought was a book and hands it to him. It's hefty, rectangular, wooden.

'What is it?' he asks.

'A Japanese puzzle box. Himitsu-Bako.'

'And what am I supposed to do with it?'

'Open it.'

A pot of water bubbles away on the hob in Stephen's modest apartment. His flat is tiny, all the rooms on top of themselves, so he can lie on his bed, cook and smell the toilet at the same time. The puzzle box sits on his bedside table. He picks it up and taps it a few times. Five sides of the box are decorated with an intricate, repetitive pattern and the top (not necessarily the top, Stephen supposes) has an image of Mount Fuji carved into the wood. Cherry blossoms in the foreground. Warm vermilion sun soaking the mountain. He spins it around in his hands and holds it up to his ear and gives it a shake. The timer buzzes on the stove and he tosses the box on his bed.

Two nights later they have arranged to meet again. Stephen knows how perceptive women can be, so he leaves work early to buy a pair of new trousers; grey, seersucker (the 'hot fabric for spring' according to the popular men's magazine that was lying around the office). Not a naturally fashionable man, Stephen looks tidy in his new trousers and pressed white shirt. The restaurant has floorboards and his noisy shoes reassure him as he steps up to the bar. This time, Erika has beaten him there and is perched on a stool.

'Hello,' she says.

Wearing red again, slim crimson blouse with fitted black jeans. Big silver hoop earrings, her black hair tied back.

'It does go faster tonight,' Stephen says. 'You look great.'

'Thanks,' says Erika, smiling.

This evening, the conversation is more intense, focused. They probe each other about past relationships. Both recently out of marriages. They agree on how difficult it is to meet people their age in London, lamenting the time pressure applied on their lives, most of their friends married, their own parents furrowing brows when the subject is brought up. And they agree that the Internet was the only option left. They don't mind that it has a stigma attached of duplicity and desperation, though they wonder what inspires people to create an online persona different to their own.

'Desperation,' Stephen suggests.

'Here's to desperation,' says Erika.

They laugh and chink wine glasses.

Last time they went back to Erika's apartment they had a cautious coffee and Stephen excused himself, not willing to seem too eager, not willing to throw himself towards a woman he had only just met. But tonight the evening masqueraded itself as something without an inevitable conclusion, as if both parties, perhaps out of maturity, or an innate caution borne from the past, played out their roles dutifully, pointlessly; accepting the dessert menu and uttering platitudes to the waiter when they passed, Stephen offering to drop Erika home in a cab, until finally, on the stoop of Erika's apartment in Chelsea, their illusions dissolved into a frantic series of lustful acts, starting right there outside the building and continuing until both of them were asleep on her giant mahogany bed, a sheet draped over the two of them, carelessly, abstract.

'Did you open the box?' Is the first thing Stephen hears in the morning.

'Hmmm?'

'The Himitsu-Bako.'

'Not yet.'

'Have you tried?'

'Yes.'

'Well try harder.'

'Good morning to you too.'

'Stephen. It's important.'

'Okay. I'll give it a proper go tonight.'

'Good boy, Erika whispers in his ear.'

Stephen picks up the box and goes through the rigmarole of turning it in his hands and tapping at the sides. He runs his fingers over the box feeling for an edge or a latch. The whole surface feels seamless, impossible. There must be a clue in the mountain, he says to himself. He studies the indentations carefully, feeling along the grooves. He lifts it to his nose, a rich whiff of wood. And then it comes to him. The Internet. Why didn't he think of this before?

'I opened your box,' Stephen says to Erika on the telephone.

'Congratulations.'

'It was empty.'

'I know.'

'Why did you want me to open it?'

'As a test.'

'A test? To test what?'

'To test how much you want me.'

Next time they meet, Stephen is greeted with an ebullient kiss. They are at Ichiban in Soho. Erika explains that the restaurant name means 'number one' in Japan. They agree that the name is a bit presumptuous and misleading. To Stephen's untrained palate the food is unremarkable, but fine. Erika is less impressed, barking at the waitress in coarse Japanese. The waitress is defensive, confused.

'Sorry madam,' she says. 'I not speak Japanese.'

'You what?' Erika says.

'I from Korea.'

Erika turns away disgusted.

'So why did she leave you?' Erika asks Stephen.

'What?'

'Your wife. Why did she leave you?'

'I don't know. She just disappeared. No warning, no note. Nothing.'

'Really? How long ago?'

'Six months.'

'That's so terrible Stephen.'

They sit in silence until the chicken katsu appears in front of them.

They're standing outside now, Erika puffing on a cigarette.

'I have another box for you,' Erika says.

'Another one?'

'Yes.'

She rustles in her handbag and withdraws a box similar in appearance to the other, but quite a bit larger.

'What's with the boxes?'

'The Himitsu-Bako?'

'Yes.'

'They're a family tradition. Four generations. My father has a small shed at the back of our house in Hakone. He makes all kinds of wooden puzzles.'

'Are they popular in Japan?'

'They used to be. When I was little I had them all over my bedroom and I'd fill them with coins and jewellery and make-up and whatever. But kids aren't interested in these types of things any more.'

'Did your father make the puzzles in your apartment?'

'Yes. He believes he's the only authentic craftsman left. All the puzzles are made by machines nowadays. The toy companies sell them for cheaper than my father can make them.'

'That's a shame,' Stephen offers.

'But, on the flip-side, he can make them as difficult as he likes.'

Stephen looks at the box when he returns home. It's decorated in much the same way as the previous one, but with more detail. The pattern is largely mosaic, hundreds of repeating tiles, but they cross over one another in different directions giving the impression of a patchwork quilt. The lid is decorated in the same vein, but within some tiles are tiny calligraphic carvings that seem to spell something out. Last time, after searching the Internet, he learnt that a box may be opened by manipulating small parts of it in a certain combination and that all boxes have thin horizontal panels that shift under pressure. The first box opened quite simply. He discovered three panels on either end of the box and shifted them left and right, listening to the noises they made and eventually he found the right order and the lid gave, slid open. Now, he tries the same technique and squeezes either side of the box feeling for any sort of give. He hears clicks and can move the panels, but there are more moving panels this time and there are too many different noises and too many areas of the box that can be manipulated.

A couple of days later, Stephen calls Erika.

'I can't open the box,' he says.

'Why not?'

'I don't know – I've tried everything.'

Erika sighs loudly into the receiver.

'Is it really that important?' Stephen asks.

'Well, it depends.'

'On what?'

'Whether or not you're interested in me.'

'Of course I'm interested in you. I just don't get why I have to open this silly box.'

'Stephen, it's not just about the box. It's about commitment, loyalty, intelligence.'

He groans. 'Erika, I don't have time to play games. I'm going to be at Ichiban, seven o'clock tomorrow.'

'Shall I see you there?'

'That's not even a proper test.' says Erika, disappointingly and hangs up.

Stephen is putting on his noisy brogues in his tiny apartment. He is complacent, already tired of the charade. He's not sure whether he wants Erika to be at the bar or not. Sure, she's beautiful and quirky and bright, he thinks, but hard work. Before he leaves he sits in front of his laptop and scrolls through hundreds of women's faces, adding a couple to his 'shortlist.' The Himitsu-Bako sits on his besides table. He picks it up and pops it in his satchel on the way out.

Erika is perched on a stool, sipping a Martini, when Stephen clomps into the bar. He is thinking that his noisy shoes are actually a bit conceited. She raises and gives him a light kiss on the cheek and returns to her seat. Stephen orders a lager.

'How are you getting on with the box?' she asks.

Stephen is tempted to give it up, concede defeat.

'Getting close.'

'Good. You never asked me about my husband.'

'Oh. What happened to your husband?'

'He died.'

Stephen reaches out and places a hand on Erika's shoulder.

'I'm sorry.'

'Don't be.'

'I didn't think you'd be here tonight.'

'I wasn't sure I'd come either.'

'Why did you?'

Erika sighs.

'I don't know. Because I'm looking for love. And you're the closest thing I've got to it.'

'I'm not sure if I'm supposed to be flattered by that, or not.'

They smile at each other, Stephen because of the frankness of the conversation, Erika, despite of it.

'When I got married, my father made a special Himitsu-Bako for my husband as a wedding gift. He spent hours on it, used the best wood he could find, carved his most intricate patterns yet. And he made it difficult. Normally a box requires anything from three to fifteen moves to open. The first one I gave you was something like that. Relatively simple. But this one required over two hundred moves to open.'

'Two hundred?'

'Yes. And a haiku was carved into the box in kanji. Niko-niko to o-wakai kao ya meoto hoshi . It's by Kobayashi Issa, a famous Japanese poet. Want to know what it means?'

'Sure.'

'It translates roughly as, 'Smiles beaming, on their young faces. Husband and wife stars.''

Stephen smiles.

'The 'husband and wife stars' are two lovers, Orihime and Hikoboshi, who are separated by a river of stars, the Milky Way. Once a year, on the seventh day of the seventh month, they cross the river to be together. There's a festival in Japan, Tanabata, to celebrate it. My husband and I were married during that festival.'

'That's really sweet.'

'My husband never figured out how to open the box. After he died my father told me that inside was the 'bridge' across the river. He died a week before our first anniversary.'

'I'm so sorry, Erika.'

'Tears are rolling down Erika's cheeks, thin salty rivulets. Stephen wipes some away with his finger.'

When Stephen wakes in the morning, Erika is gone. He had brought her back to his apartment after the bar, wildly drunk. She was a maelstrom of emotions; grief, anger, lust and Stephen could do little but watch the violence unfurl. She cried and wailed and tore her stockings to shreds and ripped the buttons off Stephen's shirt and rode him and slapped him and was sick in the bathroom and sobbed into his armpit until sleep sneaked up and walloped them both.

A sour smell of vomit and sex now floats around the room and Stephen shoves his face into the pillow next to him to engulf Erika's stale floral scent. He looks around for any sign of a note and isn't surprised when he doesn't find one. He checks his phone for messages. He tries to call Erika but reaches her voicemail. And then he falls back to sleep.

The box moves beneath his fingers. Thin horizontal panels shift left and right, an inch or two either way. Click click click click click. There are seven panels on each end, seven on each side. The ends of the box slide down a fraction, except the lid which remains tightly shut. As he shifts the movable parts back and forward they click, but every part moves and every part makes a noise, a Rubik's cube has forty quintillion permutations and after a while he stops trying.

Stephen is back at Ichiban. He recognises one of the waitresses (not the Korean one) and approaches her. He pulls the box from his bag and asks if she can translate the calligraphy on the lid. She takes the box and studies it for a moment and gives a rough translation.

'As I thought,' he says to the waitress. 'Thank you very much.'

Stephen wraps the box in brown paper and addresses it to Erika in black marker pen. Inside the package is a note.

> *Dear Erika,*
> *I am returning your Himitsu-Bako. I tried to open it, really tried, but I couldn't. I hope you find someone that can.*
> *Stephen.*

On his way to work he enters a post office, pays the cashier and pops the package into the satchel.

Ian Burton

Ian Burton, a published novelist, is co centre manager of Kinson Community Centre in Dorset, one of the biggest and busiest community centres on the south coast. He is also a Creative Writing tutor there. His Fiction Writers Workshop has been in continuous session, term by term, since 1988 and his students enjoy many successes. Ian believes fiction is all about people. He's a novelist at heart but loves to use short stories as a seed bed for ideas, character development and experimentation. *The Bovine Histories* is testament to that. He thinks technology has ensured the future of the short story.

The Bovine Histories

The field was beautiful, greener than any other, greener even than the field next to it. Kow-one could scarcely believe her eyes when the gate opened and the Stickman herded them into it. Her hooves disappeared into the lush green of heaven. 'We'll never eat all this,' she said happily to her nearest companion, 'never. But we can have a good try!' She hadn't realised it was Hathor next to her and lapsed into a shy silence. Hathor was the oldest of the herd, the wisest and the keeper of the Kow Histories. But she seemed pleased 'Well spoken.' And then she recited: 'Kow history the first. It is our duty to eat. Keep it safe.'

The herd began to spread out, establishing enough personal space to enable them to eat, stay apart and yet keep together.

Flattered by Hathor's response, Kow-one happily set about the task of eating the Green. She established a steady munching rhythm, breathing in the delicious scent, breathing out its wonderful song: 'This is heaven, this is heaven, this is heaven.'

Hathor interrupted once more. 'Well spoken again. Kow history the second. This is heaven: Keep it safe.'

It was beginning to look as if Hathor intended to stay with her and Kow-one felt honoured.

The herd relaxed, the song of the Green drifted into the contented morning. Their heaven-song could only be sung with the music of the Green in their mouths and the vision of it in their eyes.

But, as the day wore on, Kow-one's rhythm was broken once again by

Hathor as she asked, 'When was the last time we ate the Green?'

Kow-one looked at her blankly. 'But, Hathor you, above all, must know.'

Of course – but I am asking you – to see if you know.'

Kow-one resented the intrusion and wanted to say: 'Why ask questions? There isn't a cloud in the sky, no Stickman to worry about nor any of his evil Fangiyaps to bark at our heels and here we are asking questions!' But she couldn't, all she said was: 'This is our first Green since the Cold. We've been eating grey all through the Cold. This is our first day outside.'

Hathor nodded her head slowly. 'Good. You can remember, can't you?'

'What's remember?'

'Remember is...' Hathor cast her head about in the direction of the contented herd. 'If you went to stand next to Kow-two and asked her something about yesterday ... would she know what you are talking about? Would she 'remember'?'

Kow-one and Kow-two always stood side by side in the home-shed. And that was nice. Last night they had spoken with measured excitement about the prospect of the Green and speculated on when they would be allowed out to feast upon it.

If asked now about their talk, Kow-two would merely reply, sensibly: 'What a stupid, time-wasting question when you could be eating. Don't you like Green?'

On this most perfect of days Kow-one wished Hathor had not taught her this word remember.

Now she knew for certain what she'd only ever suspected – that she alone could remember.

Kow-one buried her nose back into the Green but now the sweetness of taste had faded. She felt cloud-saddened and denied, as if she had been thrown out of heaven. Feelings clumped together. She had to get away from Hathor, from remember, from everything. Without warning Kow-one found herself running. It didn't matter that the

Histories said, 'Kow history the third. Never run alone. Keep it safe.' She ran off alone.

The hedge came surging towards her. 'Kow history the fourth: Jump! Keep it safe.' But there was no meaning for the word 'Jump.' No understanding. It was just a law. Kow-one stopped, breathless, short of the hedge. Pain laced through her lungs. Running was bad, just as her mother had told her. Remembrance of mother mauled through her feelings. Looking back over her shoulder mother had said, 'Stay there.' The Stickman's stick beat a terrible rhythm before it could make her move away.

Kow-one's panting sounded obscene, profaning the contented song of the day, sawing through this Green heaven. The hedge she was staring at was no better than the wall back in the shed. But it was heaven, still. Breathing settled. Everything calmed until the only thing ringing in her ears was 'Kow history the fourth: Jump! Keep it safe.' The meaning of the word 'Jump' almost formed into sense but quickly faded with the calming breath. She turned away sadly from the hedge. The rest of the herd seemed small in the distance.

She took a bite of Green. It tasted good again. Another, it was almost sweet, another – and it was sweet. Steadily with each delicious mouthful, heaven approached.

Gradually, her eating song gained a second voice in harmony. Hathor was eating alongside her. Despite fearing the consequences of running alone Kow-one grudgingly accepted Hathor's company, wanting it.

Hathor said quietly, 'Tell me, why did you run? Can you remember?'

'I did not run. I do not remember running! I cannot remember anything. Who are you?' But it didn't work. Hathor's eyes told her

'You ran from the herd – why?'

Kow-one could feel the run feeling coming back but she stood firm. 'I ran because I can remember. And because I cannot eat properly with your questions stick-beating me. The song becomes wrong because you, Hathor are not in Heaven. I ran because all I want is Heaven – and we are in Heaven, up to our hooves in Green. But you won't shut up!' Kow-one was appalled at the sharpness of her own words.

Hathor looked at her for a long time but then said: 'Your mother named you well, Kow-one. She knew that one day you would become the new Keeper of the Histories and that day is here – it's today.'

'But you are the Keeper of the Histories.'

And again the long contemplative look from Hathor renewed Kow-one's respect for her.

"Why are you called Hathor? Why is there no Kow in your name?"

The unexpected question changed the look in Hathor's eyes.

Now there was something else in the deep brown dark of those eyes, something... wild. The word crashed into Kow-one's mind. It was never used – she'd heard Hathor use it just once – and she'd somehow understood. This light in the depths of Hathor's eyes was wild.

Moments passed. 'I became the Keeper of the Histories the day your mother was taken away. She was called Say-cred. She taught me the Histories. She told me to open my mind and my new name would come into being. I became Hathor.'

'What were you before?'

'I can't remember.' The wild returned to her eyes, briefly. She said: 'Eat. Let us sing the Green together. Later, I must teach you the Histories, all of them.'

And their song began again, tentative at first but growing, becoming a choir of two, resonating and responding and proclaiming the sweet-sweet taste of the Green.

When the first fleck of dusk was discovered by the light, Hathor broke into the eating-rhythm, ending the endless. She said, 'What's Kow history the first?'

Kow-one replied automatically: 'Kow history the first. It is our duty to eat. Keep it safe.'

'And Kow history the second?'

'Easy. Kow history the second. This was heaven. Keep it safe...' Her certainty faltered as she realised that Kow history the second had got stuck in the past, like a calf in mud.

She tried hard to tug it back out, 'Sorry, what I meant to say was : Kow history the second. This is heaven. Keep it safe. This is heaven. Keep it safe.'

But Hathor said, 'Not only do you remember but you learn. The rest merely recite the Kow histories, they remember very little and understand less. You were quite right the first time – this was heaven but you must not tell the others. This was heaven. Kow history the second. Keep it secret.'

Kow-one couldn't bare much more of this. 'Hathor, please don't talk this way. Let me go back to the herd. I made a mistake that's all. This is Heaven. That's all there is to remember. Kow history the second. This is heaven. Keep it safe. See! I got it right this time. I got it right!'

But it was as if she hadn't spoken because Hathor ground on: 'And what is Kow history the third?'

Kow-one calmed and replied dutifully: 'Kow history the third. Never run alone. Keep it safe.'

'And Kow history the fourth?'

In the long, slow silence, heaven sounds drifted from the distant herd. Bird song chanted war, bickering and peckering. Somewhere a fox terrier tested the time of day with a tentative bark. And all Kow-one wanted to do was eat just a little more before it was time for the home-shed.

But the question came stick-beating again: 'And what is Kow history the fourth?'

A breeze came combing through the Green, smelling on the nose, a smell full enough to taste.

'And what is Kow history the fourth?'

At last Kow-one answered, 'Kow history the fourth. Jump! Keep it safe.'

Hathor nodded and said, 'Good. I will tell you what Jump! is but you alone must know this – not the others...'

'And you,' Kow-one interrupted.

'I won't be here much longer. Listen carefully. Jump! is what you didn't do when you ran at the hedge. Jump! is what you wanted to do. Kow history the fourth. Jump! Keep it safe. Keep it safe from the others. When I am gone you must look for calves – your own or someone else's – and you must decide which of them is to be the next Keeper of the Histories. Now tell me, what is Kow History five? Quickly!'

Kow-one's answer was involuntary: 'Kow history the fifth. Remember. Keep it safe.'

'One day, when you've come all the way back down the road to this day, again – you must teach the Histories to the calf you have chosen just as I am teaching you now. And there are more Histories to learn yet!'

'But there are only five Histories!'

'There are eight.'

'What's eight? What are you talking about?'

Hathor looked at her and said quietly, 'Today is all the heaven I have left. There is not time to teach you how to count so that's one more thing lost but there isn't enough time to teach you everything.'

Momentarily, Kow-one saw beyond the renewed wild in Hathor's eyes and met with such sadness that she gave out an involuntary bellow of desolation. In the distance some of the herd looked idly in their direction. But Kow-one's bellow did little more than ripple the blue and Green silks of heaven and time continued apparently undisturbed.

Hathor resumed eating but Kow-one could not join in. Pits of dusk were dancing with each other in the air. Hathor looked up again. 'If there was no 'remember' there would be no pain.'

And this was so true it was as if the great sky above was heaving in a tumult of blues. Kow-one looked up at the calm yet terrifying blue sky and bellowed out, trying to be rid of understanding and remembrance.

Suddenly Hathor asked: 'What's Kow history six?'

'What's six? There is no history six. There are Five Kow histories! Five!'

'Answer me!' Her anger made Kow-one move a step away. 'WHAT'S KOW HISTORY SIX?'

Kow-one said, 'I do not know. You haven't yet taught me Kow History six!'

The long pause was charged with uncertainty. 'Haven't I?'

Kow-one shook her head and realised for the first time in her young life that Hathor's memory was fallible.

Hathor seemed about to say something more but sounds from the herd warned them that the Stickman and a Fangiyap were approaching the herd. Involuntarily they began to trek back to the others. Ahead, the Fangiyap was dancing to the Stickman's cry, nipping at the heels of anyone on the fringe. Flustered, the herd was closing ranks, all trying to avoid the edges.

As they walked along, Hathor said, calmly, quickly: 'And here is Kow history six. This is not true heaven. Kow history the sixth. Keep it secret. Say it.'

Kow-one struggled to remember the words. When she remembered them they stuck at her lips, refusing to be spoken. 'This is not true heaven. Kow history the sixth. Keep it secret.'

They paused, looking at one another, still a little away from the herd.

'Good. And now to Kow history the seventh: The road to our true heaven is perfumed with the panic-shit smell of fear. Keep it secret.'

Kow-one wanted to stop and think but all she could do was commit history to memory. They reached the edges of the herd. The Stickman prodded them.

Her mother had been standing on the road to this other 'heaven'. 'Do not follow me.' She could remember everything, the smell, the soft breeze in her mother's hair, the beat of the stick

The stick bit. Kow-one cursed remember.

As they ambled towards the home-shed, she realised that Hathor was falling behind. She paused. The way Hathor was walking, it was as if there was mud on the ground not dust.

Instinctively Kow-one knew to keep the Stickman's gaze from her.

She walked back a step or two placing herself between them. The Stickman and the dancing, barking Fangiyap immediately set about Kow-one but she let them, drawing their attention and ignoring the 'gonna-eat-you' boast of the Fangiyap.

Hathor caught up. They walked on. Outside the home-shed the bottleneck gave them precious moments alongside each other.

'Thank you,' said Hathor. 'I am sick. I should have confided in you before this day. Today is too late. I cannot remember Kow history eight. I cannot remember!'

'You must.' Kow-one was surprised to hear the urgent coldness in her own voice.

Hathor began to cry. 'I can't, I can't! My legs hurt. I feel sick.' She was reversing away.

The Stickman saw her and yelled at the Fangiyap who sprang towards Hathor and sank its teeth into her leg. Her screaming bellow threatened to spook all the others as they tried to look over their shoulders at the trouble.

Kow-one turned her back on the Fangiyap and back-kicked it perfectly in the soft underbelly. It had to let go of Hathor to yelp. Hathor staggered back into line. 'Do not get into trouble for me. You are too precious. I remember Kow History Eight now. History the eighth: the Stickmen kill us. They kill us and eat us. Keep it secret. Let the others enjoy their heaven. The next history would be nine, remember that. History the ninth...'

As they were moving into the cool shadow of the home-shed Kow-one, her voice unwavering and strong, rising up from all the turmoil inside her said: 'There is a History Nine from today. History the ninth: Remember the wisdom of Hathor.'

The wild in the glance of Hathor's eyes was tempered with love.

They were being forced apart in the home shed. 'The next History is ten. History the tenth. Choose it carefully. Choose a new name for yourself – they will accept you – when I am gone.'

Kow-one said, 'Thank you.'

Hathor mud-walked away across the unslippy floor. How long would it be before a Stickman's eye noticed what all in the herd could see that evening in the home-shed?

Kow-one found herself abandoned to memories old and new. All Kow-two could talk about was the Green, the Green, the Green, harmonising with the others cudding through their contented song.

She must choose a new name for herself. Her mother had been called theKow. Kow-one closed her eyes and her new name came to her. K-now. She would be called K-now and her search for the next Keeper of the Histories would begin tomorrow – in the Green. Another Heaven probably lay beyond the hedge. Jump! might have taken her there but now... The thud of Hathor's collapse to the floor spread alarm through the home-shed. Only K-now was silent, bewildered not by the panicky noise but by the wet gathering in her eyes.

John Fairweather

John Fairweather has a beautiful fiancé and a beautiful son. He has spent the last year in Coimbra, Portugal. *Dressing for Chess* is only his second ever completed short story and he feels delighted and very lucky that it has been published. He is writing every day now and will shortly return to sunny Birmingham in the UK.

Dressing for Chess

It's 4am when the man in the purple dress calls. I get up slowly, get myself balanced on my feet, using my thumb and my index finger I wipe the bits of sleep from eyes and flick it on the floor – it's my floor, I'll clean it later. I walk downstairs without turning on any lights. I'm heading for the kitchen. I know the phone will keep ringing, it will ring until I answer it; and so, there is no hurry. I open the fridge and open up a cold beer. It refreshes my mouth and the coldness of the beer refreshes my brain. I move into the lounge, grab the phone and sit down on the sofa. I have one of those cordless phones that answers as soon as you pick it up, but there is no need to talk straight away, I know the man will wait.

'Tony.'

He doesn't wait as long as I thought.

'Yep, it's me.'

'It's 4am.' The man in the dress always states the obvious; it is like his calling card, if it's raining he will say, 'Tony it's raining.'

'It is 4am,' I respond, 'how's your cat? Marbles is it?'

'He's dead Tony, died last Wednesday. I'm wearing my purple dress.'

'I'm wearing nothing, after all its 4am. I was in bed.' I'm not being grumpy I just feel the need to also state the obvious.

'Were you dreaming Tony?'

'I can't remember.' An honest answer; I can't remember if I was dreaming or not. Normally I dream the same dream most nights, that I'm alone in a supermarket, wandering up and down the aisles looking for gravy granules. They're never in the same place and I can never find them, so I walk from the meat section, to the tins, past the cereal, I always pick up an apple when I go past the fruit section and start munching, after all there is no one there to tell me not to and dreams make me hungry, but this time as I said I can't remember. A Kylie Minogue song pops into my head, well at least I think it's Kylie, I start to sing down the phone:

'I think we're alone now, there doesn't seem to be any one around.'

'That's Tiffany.'

'Tiff-a who.'

'Tiffany the song you're singing.' The man in the purple dress continues to speak about Tiffany, I'm not really listening, I drink my beer, sipping at first and then gulping as my body gets used to the fizz of it. I start daydreaming or nightdreaming maybe, either way I'm awake and thinking. I started to think about the first time the man with the purple dress called. It was in the morning I was on my way to work, he called I answered and all he said was, 'Hi, I'm wearing a purple dress,' I hung up of course, marked it down on a long list of bizarre events and went about my day. He was a funny anecdote at work that day, a good morning joke for the girls at the office. It was a few days before he called again. I was a bit drunk, I'd been out for a few drinks with some friends just before midnight. I was watching some football highlights and thought why not I'll chat to the crazy guy. 'So is it a nice purple dress, strapless, low-cut?' I remember asking these questions but not the answer, it turned out the man in the dress was actually entertaining, he seemed to know a lot of facts about all sorts of things, so sometimes I just listened as he rambled, if it was something interesting I'd be switched on, it was like spending ten minutes with Wikipedia. The times when I wasn't interested, like now, I'd just switch off and sip a cold beer, or watch telly. He was never invasive with his questions but every so often I'd tell him personal things about myself and he would do the same, I always missed out details such as my address, the company I worked for and he would never ask. He didn't even seem that weird after a while, just a bit nerdy, full of his facts and always stating the obvious. It was a bit like having a crazy uncle or I used to picture him as a crazy aunt, sat in a big chair, in his big purple dress, with his big purple rinse hair. Maybe he was bald I never asked and the subject never came up. After a while I just became used to him, even friendly with him. I worked a stressful job, was underpaid, worked a lot of hours and spent most of the rest of my time in the pub, watching football and chatting to friends. At work he was always something to chat about in the morning, my boss would always say 'Did the man in the dress call?' I'd say yes or no, other colleagues would say 'Why don't you just change your number?' My response was always 'I'll just give him your number instead,' and then they would go quiet. He calls twice sometimes three times a week always at different times. I never mind being woken up, as I said my job's stressful, but I've been doing the same thing for two years now, I can do my work half asleep. My girlfriend moved out a year ago so there is just me, it's not like I'm lonely, I've got friends, I'm not shy, I go out, just mostly to the same places, so I guess I've just got time on my hands and sometimes the purple dress man fills that time.

He is still rambling about Tiffany, I'm still sipping my beer; he pauses so I ask him about his cat, its been sick for a while and although he doesn't sound troubled by its death, I'm sure he had feelings for the feline, or why else would he mention it. 'Did you take Marbles to be put down?'

'Yeah, I had to, little mite had no sense of balance anymore, could hardly walk, I'll miss him, but it's a cat so you never expect them to be around for ever, they're a bit like girlfriends really.' This is the first time the man in the purple dress has ever approached the subject of girlfriends. There seems like no reason this should be a taboo subject, after all we're just two guys chatting, even though he's wearing a dress and I'm naked and drinking beer, the phone separation, that line between us, is long. Let's say that distance makes any subject, at least so far, safe to talk about.

'Do you have a girlfriend, or been seeing anyone lately?'

'Yeah Tony, I was dating a girl for a couple of months, she ended it last week, over the phone, said the relationship wasn't really going anywhere, I asked her where she envisaged two months of dating should go, she didn't really respond, just said I wasn't serious enough for her, so I became serious. I told her she was wasting her life in her job, that she could do with losing a few pounds and that her fringe made her face look pointy. She hung up.'

I was sipping beer and it dribbled down my chin as I laughed.

'What about you Tony, any girls on the horizon?'

'I don't have time at the moment,' I lie, I'm chatting to a guy in a dress at 4am of course I have time, 'works a bit crazy, we have a few new accounts , all of which are large accounts, I had a long relationship that ended last year. She used to live with me, not sure she would have appreciated your phone calls at 4am.'

'Why did she leave?'

'You know what I don't know anymore, I've spent so long thinking about why she left, that I've forgotten.'

'Like a game of chess?'

'What?'

'You think of the first move you could make, then you start looking at every piece on the board, moving it forward and backwards in your head, with each piece you think what if I did this and then what if I did that and then when you've finally finished analysing every possible move, you forget the most important thing, what your first move was, what your first idea was, that's normally the right one after all. Do you still miss her?'

'Yeah every now and again, there is even some of her clothes and stuff still here, I should throw it out but I'm lazy I guess.'

'You should get out more Tony, go meet someone new, after all it's 4am and you're chatting to a guy in a dress.'

He's right of course. 'You're right, goodnight.'

'Night Tony.' He hangs up the phone before I do. I finish my beer and go to the fridge to open another one, its cold now, not just the beer, but me also, I'm shivering. I pop the beer down on the table and head upstairs to get some clothes, turning the light on on my way upstairs, its weird I always turn the light on when I go upstairs but never on my way down, a stupid habit. I head to the bedroom and open up the wardrobe in search of my dressing gown, to its right are some clothes my ex left and my eye is caught by a white dress with red flowers, I'm not sure what the flowers are but I know they're not roses. I take the dress off its hanger and lay it on the bed. After looking at it for a while I take it and slide it on, it's a loose fitting summer type dress, flowery with straps and it fits, not like my suit I wear to work, but it fits. I look in the mirror, thinking it will remind me of my ex, it doesn't and I just look silly. Oh well at least I'm not cold anymore. I head back down stairs and pop myself on the sofa and drink my beer.

There's a movie on, some late night TV movie that no one is awake to watch, except maybe me, I'm up, I'm a little bit tipsy in a white flowery dress, watching a film that even if people were awake they wouldn't want to watch. The film's halfway through and it's about a wedding to be, the actress playing the bride reminds me of Helen, that's weird that's the first time in a while I've actually even thought her name, normally I just think ex. Then the strangest thing happens. I can smell her. It's like one of those adverts where they use food smells to remind you of your mum's home cooked stew, it's like gravy granules, that stock cube advert where the family are all happy once the food is served. I can unquestionably smell her. I shove my nose deep into the dress I'm wearing, taking a big gulp of the smell. Her smell fills my lungs with memories, all memories of the good kind. I start remembering when we first met, that first date everything it all floods back to me. It's like the dress is feeding my veins a drip full of feelings and thoughts. I reach for the phone and dial her number and then I hang up just before it starts to ring, its 5am, your ex, she's ex again, doesn't want to talk to you. I put the phone down finish my beer and pick up the phone again. I choose a number at random, picking the area code for Northampton, I don't know anyone that lives in Northampton. I dial the number, it rings ten times and a man answers with a tired voice, 'Hello.' 'Hi, I'm wearing a flowery dress,' he hangs up the phone, I remember the number and jot it down on a piece of paper and go up to bed, wearing the dress I fall asleep straight away, I'll be up again in two hours for work. I dream about the supermarket, it's empty except for me, I walk down an aisle searching for the gravy granules, this time the search doesn't take long, I find the gravy granules next to the stock cubes and the salt and pepper.

Niven Govinden

Niven Govinden is the author of novels *We Are the New Romantics* (Bloomsbury) and *Graffiti My Soul* (Canongate). His stories have appeared in *Five Dials, First City, Time Out, 3:AM, BUTT, Shortfire Press* and on BBC Radio 3.

Marseille Tip

His trunk is roughly handled at every stage. Each conductor, driver, porter and ferry hand has dragged, lugged and in several cases, kicked it around, as if it is no more precious than a deflated football. At the final stop, the quayside in Marseille, it is entrusted into the care of a boy from the boat-line, no older than fifteen, who jokingly offers to carry both the trunk and Senneevasen provided the tip is big enough.

The boy's naked back is marked with claret and aubergine-coloured bruises, the muscles in his arms and chest tight and ripped liked a circus strongman. In spite of all his assurances, which only come once payment has been received, he too dumps the trunk from one trolley to another with a sickening crack, killing any last hope that the china he has so carefully packed as a gift for his mother will emerge unscathed.

'Business or pleasure, sir? Your fine suit tells me that your voyage is for business.'

His accent suggests he is from the Congo or another inland African country. Has to be, his eyes glitter towards the sea with something like love. Even to Senneevasen, who comes from the coast, the Mediterranean that day possesses an intensely azure, shimmering magic he hadn't recognised on his last visit to this same quayside ten months earlier.

Then, he had been in too much of a hurry to reach England to appreciate anything. Now, he wonders briefly whether a life can be made somewhere along this coast, whether a diet of sun, fish and vine fruits can pan out into something respectable and not foolish.

Other men, bewitched with sun-madness and brought back to life by the urgent, hypnotic pulse that runs though Marseille, would have their heads turned by the abundance of food and the fulsomeness of the women and rethink their plans. Senneevasen is not one of those men. Ten months in England has knocked all the adventure out of him. Any romantic receptors that may have lain dormant in a young man of his age are dead. It will take more than foreign sunshine and good living to restore him.

'You are early. The boat does not leave for another three hours.'

'I didn't want to miss it.'

'Your trunk will be fine here and I can show you somewhere to eat. Not hotel cuisine, but good and cheap. You will be well looked after.'

Senneevasen holds aloft the vegetable tartine, which has been sweating under his arm since he picked it up from a stall outside the train station. The boy nods, acknowledging its talismanic presence: cheaply bought local food warding off rascals and tricksters.

'I understand, Sir,' he concurs, 'but let me show you a quiet place where you can sit in the shade. Even though we are brothers and used to the sun, it is far too hot today, no? I would not wish sunstroke on you before you have even boarded the boat.'

This too involves reimbursement, but only a ten franc note, the last of such bills he carries on him. Everything else will be drawn from the sealed envelope holding Travellers Cheques inside his jacket pocket.

In this instance, the boy takes payment reluctantly, as if it's foisted upon him by a well-meaning Elder; which he is, of a kind: Brothers-of-the-English-Speaking-Ex-Colonies in lands far from their own. They need to look out for one another, whatever bad habits they have accrued on the way: him, with his Empire-taught reserve ingrained so deeply, he fears he will never break from it; the boy, with his wily eagerness and dependence on tips.

He is led away from the passenger liners and the other men in fine suits, to a quieter area, where there are fewer dockers and less of the terrifying machinery, trolleys, forklifts and cranes that threatened to bear down upon him when he arrived. As they approach the entrance to one of the warehouses lining the quayside, the boy is called away by one of the porters.

'Inside there, Sir. No, the next one, Reunion Exports. You will find somewhere to sit there. There is very little light, but it is cool. You will be comfortable. Have you matches? You will need matches to guide yourself. Take these. No charge, Sir. Brothers should be able to exchange gifts, no? The office has closed for the day, so you will not be disturbed, but if anyone asks, say Lagos Boy sent you to avoid any misunderstanding. I will fetch you when boarding commences.'

The warehouse is as billed: dark, cool and empty of goods. His only companions are infrastructure, caged grills lining floor to ceiling (he guesses, matchlight unable to provide vision much beyond head height), trolleys and humps of newspapers and other discarded packaging. Further from the safety of the door is a table and set of four chairs, presumably for the watchman, which he finds with some difficulty, burning his fingers on the matches left by the boy.

The chairs are narrow, splintered at the back and without cushions, but they are placed in such a way that he is able to sit on one and rest each foot on another, in a position that is mostly comfortable, so long as he does not move excessively.

The coolness of the room envelops him, something like a bath and the darkness is palpable. Hidden away from the chaos of the port, he lets his shoulders fall and closes his eyes. It is the most relaxation he has known since leaving his tiny room in the house on Battersea Park Road. A day and a half's trudging and rattling has brought him to this private, welcome darkness.

Senneevasen is leaving England because he was a failure there and also because of some trouble with a girl. He is returning to India where he hopes to get married and settle down into the life his parents wished him to escape.

By returning, everyone will know that he has achieved very little in his time abroad. The shame of this will follow him around from the moment the boat docks into Bombay, like the smell of bad fruit past its prime and starting to rot. But he hopes that in time he will make something of himself, a period of unqualified success, where tales of his previous failures will be disbelieved and fall into legend.

The tartine, having sweated down into something inedible, is abandoned after the first bite. In the distance he hears the hissed drumming of a leaky faucet, but he is loath to use up his few remaining matches to find it, in spite of his dry mouth. He fears running out of light on the return journey and being trapped amongst the crates, like a pinball blindly shot through a series of dead ends.

Hunger suddenly grips him, as it always does, in the absence of good food. His entire time in England was marked by such hunger. He wonders whether he should find the boy and get directions to the place he'd talked of so highly. A fortifying plate of couscous and fish is just what he needs. Perfect, in fact.

He does not wish to board the boat weak and light-headed. In his eagerness to leave England and the threatening girl behind, he has forgotten about the choppiness of the sea and the butterflies that breed in his stomach, seeping into his guts, until his legs connect to dry land again.

It is this condition that brought on his sea-sickness, which he suffered from throughout the first week of the voyage. During that time he was mocked by passengers and crew alike, until his patience was finally worn down after an incident in the dining room, where the sight of a cauliflower gratin being dished up made him vomit into his lap. He forced himself to find his sea legs after that humiliation.

He must have dozed briefly, sedated by the stillness of the air inside the warehouse, a stillness he knows he will not find on any boat. He is shaken awake by Lagos Boy, with a strength of wrist not solely limited to the loading and unloading of luggage. On the table lies an opened Coke bottle next to a bowl of couscous and meat.

'You eat meat? They would not give me the fish one. They are saving it for the tourists.'

'You eat. I have my sandwich.'

He points to the disintegrating log of crumb and vegetable mush on the chair seat.

'I have already eaten. Manon, the woman who cooks there, feeds me if I find any trinkets for her.'

Travellers are often in a state of fluster Portside. The noise, conflicting demands of customs officials and liner staff and the domineering stature of the gangway, a stairway to either hope or disappointment, led them to be careless, dropping purses, sunglasses and badly fastened jewellery. Lagos Boy takes the first sweep of pickings to Manon. He tells Senneevasen how he once received a whole lobster in exchange for a bulky box gramophone with two Charlie Parker records packed in the lid.

'You have not mentioned your business in Bombay.'

'I thought you only carried bags?'

How effortless to be lofty whilst taking advantage of another man's shelter and eating his food. He has been asked this question too many times on his journey down to Marseille and still unable to answer satisfactorily, is sick of doing so. But he catches himself on seeing the boy's eager face crumple into hurt and reminds himself that he is just a child, however well developed. He must not treat others the way he has been treated in England, fearful, mean-spirited and with condescension.

'I am going there to start a business,' he says, gently.

He has been practising this alibi in his head ever since his life in England became untenable. Now uttered to flesh and blood, he marvels how this flimsy sentence takes weight and becomes believable.

'Something grand, eh? You would not leave London for something any person could do.'

'How did you know I was from London?'

'Eat your couscous. Manon may say differently, but I do not think it tastes as good when it grows cold.'

'I never told you where I was from.'

'All the fine men from England come from London. There is nowhere else…and I read it on your luggage.'

He cannot speak for the next few moments for the couscous is that good. It doesn't matter that he is unable to identify the meat. Lagos Boy has pronounced it chicken, but he tastes something different, less dense than pork, but white and full bodied like rabbit. Whatever it may be, it is delicious.

The boy watches anxiously, awaiting approval. So far he has not given praise and understands this is what the boy covets, recognition that he has done good, haloed by the smallest of coins pressed into his palm.

'You must know all the best people if you come from London.'

'Some,' he says modestly, for aside from the kindness the fiancée of his former landlord initially showed him, there has been little opportunity between studying and working nights as a bottle washer at Wandsworth dairy to get to know anyone.

'There are fine people travelling our lines also, but most do not wish to speak to me. The Captain of one of your cricket teams was very pleasant, however. He signed a cricket ball.'

'You like cricket?'

'Football. We play at night after the boats are loaded.' And after a time, anxiously, when no affirmation comes. 'You don't like sport?'

His work colleagues had the same question too. Sennevasen's sporting knowledge is scant, reliant on the occasional evening newspaper left behind on the bus. Prose related to economics was all he was prepared for. He knew about the World Cup, but the fractured league system and the complicated nature of the game bewildered him. He could have picked up more from the radio at the dairy, immersed himself the same way he'd developed his English, but the noise from the bottle washing machines was too noisy to pick up anything.

His answers in those situations came to nothing, some pitiful titbit, always behind everyone else's knowledge, making him realise that knowledge of sport was as competitive as playing it. His colleagues, misunderstanding his hesitancy for aloofness, were annoyed that their efforts to include him were so readily snubbed. Consequently they nodded curtly in acknowledgement in the changing room but left him to his own devices.

' Sorry, I was just wondering why are we speaking English to each other?'

'Because you would not understand my broken French and I don't speak Hindi.'

It is that simple.

'You must know the Beatles. Did they live near you?'

'Oh yes, very near. I would see them most days when they were not touring. This couscous is excellent, by the way. You must give my compliments to your Manon.'

The Beatles lie comes easily, because in the face of hope he is used to lying; to the fiancée of his landlord with his promises of tenderness, not understanding that she would become possessive and demand more of him; to his university tutors who expected brilliance based on his entrance papers but rarely saw it; and now to the boy who wishes to be comforted by celebrity and the idea that four lads from Liverpool could forge friendship with a Brother of the English Colonies.

'If you bring my trunk I can give you a gift as way of thanks.'

'But your trunk is ready to be loaded on board the ship, Sir.'

'If you leave now it shouldn't take long. I promise the journey will be worth it.'

He snoozes again, only waking when the trunk is dropped before him; albeit with a softer landing than previously, but still with a thud that rings though their cavernous resting place. With Lagos Boy providing matchlight, he crouches down, opens the padlocked seal and rummages. Thankfully the china, wrapped individually and lodged between jumpers, socks and itchy woollen trousers (to be joyously burnt the moment he reached Bombay), is unharmed. He pulls out one of the mid-sized packages for Lagos Boy.

'A plate? Why do you give me a plate?'

'I was saving it for the museum at home, but since you have treated me so well... It is not just any plate, but one which Ringo Star has eaten from.'

Lagos Boy has been travelling on the boat lines since he was 13-years-old. The plate is riches.

'I am founding a museum for music memorabilia. I have Ringo's plate, a drumstick from Keith Moon and an old coat of Mick Jagger's.'

The big talk comes easy on a full belly and in this empty space where there is no one to account to. Big talk in the dairy would have got his head smashed in.

'Ringo's my favourite! He is the best Beatle.'

'I made chicken curry and rice one night and he ate his from this plate!'

'How do you know that it was Ringo who used this and not Paul?'

'Because only Ringo ate with me that night. The others were at a party with Peter Sellers.'

'This is a beautiful plate. I will sleep with it under my pillow.'

He realises that a museum filled with rubbish is the route out of shame, a distraction from any charges of stupidity and a wilful squandering of British opportunity. That the boy is taken by his story in a heartbeat causes a tightening deep in his chest. He sees how his family will also be taken in by these cheap objects. The Beatles have vowed never to tour again. They are only interested in Northern India, not his part. Who is there to question him?

In England, dismayed by the welcome, he blundered into silence by a series of gaffes. Now he can be the big man, successful, confident and unafraid.

He sends Lagos Boy away, with instructions to wake him at the ship's final call. He is a busy man and should not be made to wait.

Eluned Gramich

Eluned Gramich was born in Haverfordwest, Wales to a Welsh mother and German father. She has spent time in Munich, Bavaria and Bordeaux. She had the pleasure of going to school in Bristol before studying for a BA in English at Oxford. She is an amateur violinist and translator and one day hopes to be able to speak Japanese fluently. She is currently working for an Independent Publisher based in Cardigan and has been accepted on the MA course in Creative Writing at the University of East Anglia which she will be starting this year.

The Milk Jug

Boom – boom – boom says the television boom-boom the explosion goes and lights up the room in many different whites and greys. Little Maksim laughed suddenly like a dog yelping. 'Boom-boom-boom!' he said and threw his arms above his head and smiled. But the cartoon had already moved on. Now the black cat was running very fast and twisting its tail and opening its big red mouth. Little Maksim's smile disappeared quickly and his face returned to an expression of fascination at the grotesques on the screen. He watched television after school everyday until it was time for bed. The television was new (he had only been given it a year ago), but now he could not imagine a life without it. The screen lit up again and the sound of a train rattling through the monotone landscape hit the room. Choo-choo! He leaned forward on to the palms of his hand to look at the train more closely; it was tearing after the black cat. It was tearing through the fields and over bridges. Maksim, who had never seen a field or a railway bridge before, recognised it only as a cartoon world where the black cat and its friends lived and were chased by trains and explosions. In Kiev, he was surrounded by streets. There were no streets or roads in cartoons and he loved this other-world where no person could really live. He leaned back onto his haunches and watched the train groaning to a halt in a mass of grey steam. In the seconds of quiet after the train had stopped, he heard his mother moving the boxes around in the next room and talking to his grandmother. Maksim looked quickly towards the door, worried that his mother was going to come and get him. He moved nearer to the television screen and watched the figures intently, possessively remembering their movements and shapes for the night-time. Maksim gasped as music hit the room suddenly, filling it with the song he knew well and sung at school with his friends. 'Dum-dum-dah dum-di-dah,' he sang to himself. Where was the little cat and his friend now? The cartoon was rolling white letters down the black screen like snowflakes against a concrete road. He could hear his mother moving towards the door: the music had betrayed him. Quickly, he changed the channel, but it was too late.

'Maksimka. Time for bed,' she said softly. She was already wearing nightclothes: maroon slippers and a long white gown with no sleeves. Her freckles could be seen crowding her upper arms and chest in reddish clusters; there were some even below her ears, visible now that she tied her hair up in the evenings so that it would be easier to brush the next day. 'Time for bed,' she called again from the doorway. Maksim looked up at her from where he was sitting on the floor. He did not answer so that she would think he could not understand, or could not hear her. Perhaps she would give up and let him watch a little more. Recently, she had let him stay up later than usual while she spoke with grandmother and carried on with the preparations. Go and wrap up my things in brown packages, he thought. Go and wrap up the cups and plates in white tissue paper.

'Maksimka,' she said as she walked over to the television set. She switched it off and the room was silent. His ears were overwhelmed with this sudden quietness, as if the world had been muted, as if he had become deaf. 'Boom-boom-boom!' he remembered. But too late as he was led to his room by his mother's warm hands clutching his arm. Maksim was a quiet boy and did not complain when he had to go to bed. His mother would often tell him that he was a 'good little Maksim', much better than the boys in the flat downstairs who would scream and jump out at you when you turned the corner at the bottom of the stairs. 'Little horrors. Little devils,' his mother said. His grandmother, who rarely left the flat, would nod in agreement and tell a long story about her old neighbours. Such good people are hard to find, she would say at the end, looking at Maksim.

That night Little Maksim dreamt of many things. He dreamt of the big rattling train from the cartoon. He dreamt that he was standing at the very front where the smoke came out of the chimneys: he was looking at himself on the train from the grey fields in which he was standing. It is like that sometimes in dreams. He thinks: I am in the fields, but I am also on the big smoky train. His grandmother and mother were standing on the train too with brown packages strewn all around them, waving. 'Goodbye goodbye,' they said in Russian and then the train was off. Maksim's heart wrenched in his chest, wriggled in his ribcage like the maggot he had discovered in the apples at school and then leapt into his throat and then into his head causing it to split into so much pain. His entire face seemed to burn with the pain of this parting, scalded by the heat of the steam on his skin. Suddenly he was the black cat running after the train. Then he was no longer a cat but the train itself. His grandmother said to him: 'Good little Maksim. Don't stop running now. We are almost there.' Maksim immediately understood where they were going and was filled now with an unfamiliar happiness: it was the sort of nervous happiness he felt on New Years when he was given presents from members of his family he did not know. Strange uncles and aunts smiling down on him with wide-eyes, smelling of dusty old rooms and cooking oil. He opened one of the gifts in his dream and inside was a brown package and inside that was an old clock. It was broken. 'Why is it broken?' he asked. 'It's not broken,' the strangers all replied. Maksim looked at the old clock again and realised that it was not broken, but was ticking away loudly and showing the time which he could not read properly yet. The clock rang. Maksim woke up.

It was Sunday so he did not go to school. In any case, his mother had explained to him already that he would not go to school in Kiev anymore as they were moving away very soon. That is why his mother spent all day with grandmother preparing. They had already packed away Maksim's things: a few school books, his photographs and paintings, the notes he had written for his mother which said things like: 'I love you' or sometimes 'I hate you', all misspelt. They were packing up some of the things from the kitchen now. Although their flat was very small, they had managed to collect many things over the years; some of them came from the old farmhouse where grandmother used to live when she was a young girl. Maksim watched his mother and his grandmother packing the things they would need and putting the things they wouldn't need into bin bags and boxes to give away later.

'Are you hungry Maksimka?' asked his grandmother. He nodded fervently. 'Oh yes, very very hungry. 'His grandmother got up slowly from where she was sorting out the cutlery on the table and went towards the little whirring fridge in the left corner of the kitchen. She moved so slowly because her legs were bad: sometimes when she thought that no one could see her she lifted the heavy brown skirt that covered her legs and scratched her veins. Maksim, who she supposed was watching television, would sneak a glance at her legs with the same expression of fascination with which he watched the explosions on screen. He followed the blue swollen veins with his eyes up and down her legs; he saw that her ankles were swollen too and that her skin was uneven like porridge, as if under her skin lodged many little marbles. She poured milk into a plastic cup, walked back to her seat and gave it to him. 'Maksimka come and sit near Baba.' He drank his milk and splashed it over his face and onto his shirt. He wiped the milk off with his hands and walked to his grandmother and put his head into her armpit. She put her arms over his shoulders and squeezed his arm tight. When Maksim looked up, he saw the heaviness in his grandmother's face; and the lightness and glitter in her brown eyes.

Maksim was wearing the thick vest his mother had bought him the week before, so that he would be warm on the journey. It was heavy and uncomfortable and he wished he could tear it off and wear the red one instead. But all his clothes had been packed away apart from a raincoat, a pair of underpants and a pair of black socks for the next day. His mother had carefully folded and pushed the rest of his clothes into the crevices left amongst the plates and cups in the suitcases. 'We have to make sure that nothing breaks,' his mother said. Some of the suitcases were so heavy that she could not lift them. They would have some help from the neighbours to carry the things to the station, she said. 'But it will be a struggle for us when we arrive. And we do not need anymore trouble,' said his mother. So she opened the heaviest suitcase which belonged to Maksim's grandmother and began to take the things out. Grandmother stopped what she was doing and watched from where she was sitting. It was filled with old things, heavy things. First, his mother pulled out a white milk jug from the centre. Maksim had seen it before; his grandmother kept it in the glass cupboard above the kitchen table. It was different from everything else he had seen. On its handle were the faint traces of a green stem and a blue flower; faint because it had been washed so many times over the years. A bluebell, maybe. Along with the jug, his mother took out a few books, tapes and a black plastic radio that was once his grandfather's. She put all these objects carefully on the floor next to the suitcase. Then she looked up at grandmother. She looked up sadly but also sternly: Maksim recognised that look. She often looked at him this way if he had done something wrong, like when he had broken the bedroom window in the summer, or played with the bad children from the flat below. Then she looked away at the things on the floor again. Maksim glanced at his mother, then at his grandmother, then at his mother again. Their faces were cold and harsh; expressions that Maksim was unaccustomed to. There was a long silence and Maksim knew to be silent too. He continued to watch his family; he felt scared. Then his mother did something he had not seen before. She stretched out her hand and gently, brushed her mother's elbow with the tips of her fingers. His grandmother nodded then and began to polish the metal cutlery with a napkin as if nothing had happened. No word passed between them; but the objects remained on the floor and were not put back into the suitcase. Maksim finished his milk and went to watch cartoons next door.

His grandmother was very quiet in these days before the move. She did not walk around, tying and untying packages and boxes as her daughter did. She examined the American money that Maksim's mother had managed to get from some friends, but she was not as excited as her daughter was, or her grandson. Maksim knew that she was unhappy and this made him uneasy and often in his dreams he would feel this uneasiness utterly overwhelm him. Often the smoke of the train would swallow him up so that his family could not see him, swallow him up so completely that he would be left behind in Kiev all alone. Sometimes the smoke would be so thick he could not move or breathe and he would wake up coughing and crying. In the evening before the move, they sat together eating the last of the food they had left in the kitchen: bread, ham, cabbage and some butter. His grandmother suddenly smiled and nodded at Maksim, sensing that he was unsure and unhappy about the emptiness of the flat and the strange silence that had suddenly gripped his mother. 'Don't worry Maksimka. It is like your mother said, in a few days now we will be in a new country and a new place. We will have a better life there and you will go to a new school and make many friends.' The last bit she said emphatically, as if defending herself from someone who thought otherwise. 'There are many good people where we are going. You will make many friends.' Maksim was old enough to know that the smiles of confidence and happiness his grandmother gave him that evening and the next morning were false, yet they reassured him all the same.

There was no television for him this evening, as they had already sold the set to some strangers from another street. Everything was empty and cold: even his bed felt unfamiliar that night and his dreams were no longer filled with cats and trains. They were as cold and as empty as the rooms around him. They left for the station early the next day and boarded the train before noon. From the window of the train Maksim watched the broad streets of the city race past him like the spokes of a bicycle. His grandmother smiled at him and looked towards the window too. Little Maksim could not smile back but he watched his grandmother carefully. Her dark skin was illuminated by the dawn light and the sunlight played its colours on her grey hair which was carefully tied back with many metal grips. She was wearing a brown raincoat. Maksim, whose mother had gone to see to the suitcases in the baggage compartment, moved towards his grandmother and put his head on her stomach. She smelt of home and the warmth from her body embraced him and the rocking motion of the train motioned him to sleep again. Yet, from the side of the coat he felt something hard and strange press against his temples. He startled and moved away. Opening his eyes, Maksim saw a glimmer of white shine from beneath the black lining of his grandmother's coat and a thin handle with a blue flower jut out of the pocket. His grandmother only smiled and turned to watch the last greys of her city flickering past the window.

Naomi Lever

Naomi Lever was born in Milton Keynes and currently teaches English in Newcastle upon Tyne. She has written prose and poetry since she was tiny but currently gets distracted from writing by kayaking and mountain biking. One day she will get around to finishing her novel(s).

Katie's Sandpit

Katie only plays in the sandpit at school now. When it rains, she gets done by Mrs Clarkson because it's against the rules if it's wet and Gemma Lewis always tells whenever anyone breaks the rules. When it's sunny, there are others playing in the sandpit and they ruin it a little bit but Katie is used to sharing. Anyway, she always crouches in the same corner and the others have started to realise that this is the Katie-corner and they shy away from it, like a herd of gazelles billowing slowly away from a sleeping lion. Katie enjoys the thought of being a lion; sometimes she would quite like to roar, to pounce, to savage until the world goes silent.

These are the games that Katie plays: building, burrowing, burying. Games for one. She draws pictures sometimes, goats, usually, rag-coated and stump-horned, or suns like melting eyes, or houses with holes for windows. Sometimes she will write words, though her letters topple over or swap places when she isn't looking and sometimes she forgets to dot her 'i's; Mrs Clarkson doesn't mark this work though, she doesn't have a giant red pen to gouge rusty 'Spellings!' or blood-stained 'Capital letters' into the sand. These are some of Katie's secret words: hell man, allkeeder, lootnant. They are kept secret under the sand: she brushes layers over the words like yellowing lace, thin blurs full of whispers.

She carries the sand with her, not on purpose, or at least not at first, but it gets everywhere: under her nails, into her clothes, behind her ears, in the nooks of her pigtails, between her toes. Her daddy once went to the hospital with an ear infection only to be told that his ears were plugged with desert. Afterwards, he told Katie and Josh that he could hear the desert. 'Like holding a sea shell to your ear and listening to the waves crashing, you know?'

'What does the desert sound like?' asked Katie, snuggled on his knee; Josh, older, pretended not to be interested, sprawled on the carpet but so near their daddy's feet he was touching.

'Like stories,' Daddy said. 'There are the winds – scuttling winds, growling winds, idly rolling winds – and there are the sands, stirred and sifting and there are the distant cries of birds on the mountains and echoing goat bells and the grasses rustling like dry paper. And it all sounds like stories that someone is trying to tell you, but from far away or underground or secretly.'

'You're wasted as a soldier,' Mummy laughed. 'Look at their faces! Rapt!'

Katie sometimes gets sand in her ears and sometimes she thinks she can hear the desert too: straining until her neck cricks and the skin about her ears feels about to blister and peel off, she can sometimes convince herself that the tickle-itch shifting in her ear drums is really a story in the distance. At home she lies on the sofa with her cheek to the woven cushion that Daddy brought home the last time he was on leave. If she twitches her skin against the weft, there is a rough rustle that could be grasses or sands or winds. Up close, the gold and green pattern spirals and shuffles into muddles and if she squints, she can pick out slopes and dips of dunes, flat bright stretches, the smudged murk of distant mountains. When she sits up, the cushion changes back to silent flowers.

'How have you got sand into the cushion?' Mummy demanded. Her voice was cracking, scraping, like the noise Josh made scuffing his feet down the wall whenever he was angry or upset and wanted to be annoying. 'And in your reading book – and your lunchbox! What do you do?'

Katie was silent: when she was silent, Mummy would gaze at her with tired, wetly irritated eyes and huff out a strange moaning sigh and then her eyes would go blank and she would stroke Katie's hair and tug not-quite-gently on a lock of it, as though trying to pull open imaginary blinds. Then she would scrunch her nose and jerk her chin and drift away like a streak of dust motes out of the sunlight.

'The sunlight is different out there,' Daddy had told them. 'There's just so much of it – and then suddenly so little. At midday the light is pale and everything moves slowly, as though you're wading underwater in a lake of lemonade. Then in the hour before sunset it all turns golden and orange. You look at the sands and they seem to spill towards you like syrup. For an hour you squint. The horizon blurs and the world burns. And then sunset and near-instant dark – except for the moon and beneath the moonlight the sand washes silver.'

Not just silver, though this is no desert: Katie can see the sandpit in the moonlight from their classroom window and Daddy was right – it is silver. But there is also white like pearls and blue like tears.

It is Parents' Evening and Mummy and Mrs Clarkson are talking about her. After this they will go to see Miss Palmer and they will talk about Josh and it will be his turn to squirm and do the boy-equivalent of awkwardly chewing his pigtails.

'...and her literacy skills are impressive too. Although there has been a slight plateauing out in levels, but that's to be expected in these circumstances. In actual fact, I've become a little concerned about her writing. In terms of fluency, her spelling has gone a little, ah, experimental, which can apparently be a common side effect of trauma – attempts to change reality? Do stop me if this becomes too difficult?'

'No, no! No.'

'It's the subjects of her stories that worry me a little. They're all the same and it seems a rather unusual focus to seize upon. At first I thought she'd been discovering 'The Arabian Nights', but ...' Mrs Clarkson catches Katie's eyes and she fish-gulps then trout-pouts. 'Mrs Waters, I wonder if we could speak in private? It might be a little sensitive?'

Katie hates this habit of Mrs Clarkson's – making everything sound like a question. The Viking ships were called longboats? Four times three is twelve? You must use a capital letter at the start of a sentence? The uncertainty is unsettling – what's the real answer? Or if it is a question, how should Katie answer? Yesnomaybedon'tknow, words squashed into a lump of nonsense, incoherence bordering on hysteria.

Mummy looks a little bewildered too and maybe a little hysterical, but that is normal now. 'I see – um – Josh, would you take Katie out into the playground? Please? Play hopscotch or something?'

Questioning is contagious; Josh asks, 'Do I have to?'

'Be my little man, Joshy.'

Josh huffs and puffs, but the m-word gives him a strut and he bundles Katie into her coat and bustles her to the door. As they leave, Katie hears, "She's developed a bit of an obsession…"

Outside, the night touches her face like glass: dark, cold, fragile. Black branches tilt the clouds; the moon leans close like a face into a mirror. Josh slopes over to the climbing frame and dangles upside down from his knees; he is tall enough now to reach down (or up, surely?) and write in the bared earth. Katie used to like the climbing frame, but she only plays in the sandpit now.

The sand is cold as she sits down, like getting into a bath with all her clothes on. She dips her fingers in and lets the sand drizzle onto her tights and then lets some more. She carries on until she has buried her legs entirely. And then she lies back, careful not to let her toes nudge free.

This is what Daddy saw: vast dark, a peering pale moon and sand like silver water falling away all around. This is what he felt: sand, faintly damp, surprisingly solid but nonetheless crawling into his clothes, sharp grit chafing his collar. This is what he heard: shifting, whispers, hushed stories somewhere behind his head.

Left alone, Katie lifts handfuls of sand and drops them onto her stomach until she can feel their weight pushing her down, deeper into the sand. It does not hurt yet; she suspects that it never will. She can only imagine and all she does is imagine: as she pushes closer to the sand, a red stain spreads and the whispers seep closer through the chill.

Miha Mazzini

photo by Robert Kruh

Miha Mazzini is the author of 23 published books and his work has been translated into 8 languages and has been selected for many anthologies. He is a screenwriter of 2 award-winning feature films and the writer and director of 4 short films. He has an MA in Creative Writing for Film and Television from The University of Sheffield. He lives in Slovenia.

The Flies

Half asleep, he waited for the alarm clock to go off, listening to a fly bumping into a window. He knew he mustn't move if it landed on him. I mustn't, I mustn't, he kept repeating and sank down until Sabine gently shook his arm and brought him back. He helped her dress Grette and walked them both to the door. After locking it, he moved to the windows and cracked them open. He didn't see the fly. After yesterday's storm the summer had cooled down enough to leave the windows ajar. Berlin flats: there wasn't this much room available for this rent anywhere he had been previously sent.

He went to the toilet, shaved, took a shower and stared long into the mirror without really seeing himself. Sometimes he became stuck like this even with Sabine and Grette at home and he was always embarrassed afterwards, but his wife pretended she hadn't noticed, while his daughter had never known him to be any different.

He knelt down in the right direction without praying. The walls needed whitewashing. Sabine planned to fix up the flat during her leave. Outside, retired women rattled their carts over Zossener Straße as they went to market place.

On Tuesdays he made steak, but while he was waiting in line at the butcher's, looking at the cut, hung, packed and displayed meat, he recalled the buzzing and leaned forward unconsciously, as if he had bad eyesight, to look for the flies. They should have been skimming over the pink surface of the meat, crossing the muscle lines, the layers of trimmed fat, changing direction, taking off, stopping, rubbing their legs together.

He decided it was better to go to the fish market. Vacuum-packed calamari in his hand, he waited at the vegetable stand for potatoes. They were packed in nylon bags and each one he picked from the pile weighed exactly five kilos. German orderliness never ceased to amaze him. In the late socialist Yugoslavia where he had grown up, you never bought just a kilo of something; you snatched up whatever appeared in the shops, because you never knew when it would turn up again. Those were not shops but hunting grounds – you entered them wondering what you would catch, if anything. And here: so many bags, all weighing precisely the same. And no flies anywhere. He couldn't remember if they buzzed around Yugoslav shops. Probably. How long would Germany have to disintegrate for them to appear here?

The pensioner in front of him tried to show her independence by counting the money by herself, shuffling through her wallet, long and wrong. The entire line, including the cashier, waited silently. This wouldn't have happened in our country, he thought. The woman's hands began to shake and she finally pushed the coins away and the cashier took over the counting. She quickly extracted the right amount, but it took the woman a while to put the remaining coins back into her purse. 'I don't know what's wrong with me today,' she said.

It's what will be wrong with you every day until you die, he thought and more so.

He looked at the reflection of the line in the shop window – a blur of grey hair. He found his head only because it was the only male one and stuck out high above the others. Germany is a land of old ladies, at least in the mornings. I mustn't get stuck, I mustn't. 'Good morning,' the cashier said casually.

He waited at a crosswalk for a line of kindergarten children to cross. They were holding on to a rope, each by his or her own handle, obediently letting an aged punk lead them. He saw the likes of this fellow often in his neighbourhood – the mohawk haircuts, which had looked menacing the night before, now just orientation points for the children. Judging by their faces, at least half of the children were Turks, some girls wearing headscarves, some blacks, some Asians, a minority of whites and some he couldn't place. His eyes should have been scanning the group for Grette, but instead they fixed on the rope. Was there a fly? Strange, this is strange. Why today? Was the buzzing this morning only a dream, or did I really hear the fly and now it won't leave me alone?

He spread the potatoes on the table, pulled a knife out of the block and placed a green bag made of special plastic for biodegradable waste nearby. How long had engineers tried to develop something that would last forever? When they finally invented plastic, it quickly took over the world, but of course it had one fault: it wasn't degradable. So they had to invent a different version. He held it in his hand and felt the fragments from the past surfacing. He got stuck and could not tell how much time had lapsed.

He dug his face into his hands.

A fly landed on his forearm. I mustn't move. He opened his eyes: darkness, some pink blurs where his fingers didn't mesh properly. The creature slowly moved along his arm. I mustn't move. He felt its every leg on his skin; his left arm ached to strike, the right one wanted to move and scare it off. The fly stopped. Breathe as little as possible, he must breathe as little as possible. He pressed his palm against his nose, rasping in breath. Slowly, slowly he removed his hands. The fly moved upwards, reached the elbow crease and stopped.

But it's not, he told himself, it's not, I mustn't move, I mustn't move, but I can have a look, a look.

He released the pressure of his hands and slowly moved his head to the right so that his eye appeared between his forefinger and thumb.

He didn't see the fly. He felt it going back towards his wrist but didn't see it.

He remained still until it flew away. Then he spread his hands on the table and examined the path the fly made again and again. The normality of the skin bothered him.

So, it's the nerves, the doctors would say. Whenever they mentioned nerves, he pictured thin, leafless branches stretching inside him. He went to the bathroom and scrubbed the skin that the fly had crawled over with soap. Nothing like this had ever happened to him. What if it happened again? On the way back he reached out for the door frame and got lost in time again.

Sabine worked longer on Tuesdays, so he went to pick up Grette from kindergarten. She immediately sat down in her Barbie doll corner and started playing. Girls seemed strange, or was it only her? Boys... boys.

His boys.

(Sead . . . Safet)

He sat down at the table – it was time to peel the potatoes. He took the knife and picked up the first one, staring at it for a long time. There wasn't a speck of dirt on it, as if it had never been in the ground. He cut into it and revealed its whiteness.

Grette sneezed and said gesundheit to herself. He looked over at her. A German, I have produced a German. After everything ... a German. Blonde, blue-eyed, fair-skinned, my own child devoid of me. Pure Sabine, only much more beautiful. Sabine had always called herself a mousy-looking woman and for the longest time he really hadn't noticed her. He reported at the office as he was told, diligently following the rules for asylum holders; Sabine had made all the moves. He was waiting in line one day and noticed her looking at him strangely. She's going to give me trouble, he thought. She didn't, but as he put away his passport, he found a piece of paper sticking out of it with a phone number. He had no desire to call, but he fell asleep in the afternoon – he shouldn't have, afternoon naps always end in nightmares! – and when he jumped up all sweaty and screaming, he needed to hear a human voice, break out of the darkness, so he dialled the number.

He let Sabine lead him through their relationship and she let him get stuck now and then. Physically he functioned okay, as long as she worked him long enough and provided that he closed his eyes. And now a German girl was playing with Barbie dolls right before him. From the very beginning, Grette had always reached out for him, especially when she was learning to walk. His first impulse was to move away, but then he would force himself to wait for her hands. The delay made him an awkward guardian and Grette fell a lot. When she was two, Grette's favorite thing was to sneak up and kick him in the crotch as hard as she could. That lasted a couple of months before it stopped. Now she absorbed herself with Barbie dolls and shut him out. He expected Sabine to throw him out of the apartment one day, but she treated him kindly and gently, as if he was her patient. Perhaps I'm a good cook, he considered, without the slightest hint of humour.

'Du bist sehr schön,' Grette said to a combed Barbie doll as she placed it in a little pink armchair with a sigh.

A German, there's none of me in her, none of my features, none of my history, none of my past. I haven't given her anything; she's got nothing to do with me.

She's safe.

A fly settled on the back of his hand. I mustn't move. He looked down but didn't see it, only felt it crawling toward his wrist. When the second fly landed on his neck, he almost flinched. Then the third, the fourth; he stopped counting. He stared blankly into the wall above Grette as flies crawled over him.

I mustn't move.

He slowly closed his eyes and tried breathing as softly as possible.

Bright redness, it had to change into darkness, evening, night; then he could sneak away.

He just mustn't move.

Flies, everywhere, on his forehead, on his twitching eyelids, he couldn't control himself. Did they see him? Were they above him? A moment ago someone said something about gasoline, but there was no one there now, it was hot, they went for a beer, the excavator broke down or they didn't have one, they were shovelling the earth, they should have left enough of them alive to bury their own, he heard them say, someone thought singing would help but others didn't join in, sometimes they came so close he could smell liquor but mostly blood, blood, blood. Excrement, urine, sweat, every drop smelling of fear, blood, blood, blood. The heavy stench of earth. Black, full of roots. He didn't want to smell, he didn't want to hear, he only wanted to live and that's why he kept telling himself I mustn't move I mustn't move, the flies were crawling over him, under his T-shirt, under his trousers, they were crawling everywhere, someone's arm was lying across his face, across his mouth, they won't see I'm breathing, just no gasoline, don't let them find any gasoline, night, night is coming, I mustn't move, I mustn't move, blood is trickling from the arm, flies are sucking it from his skin, then the blood stops, the bodies on which he's lying are getting stiff. Wife and kids, are Ines, Sead and Safet beneath him? No, no, he mustn't think, dead, dead, dead, he mustn't think. I mustn't move, I mustn't move. Flies, flies, flies countless legs on him, crawling over him, I mustn't move. (Earlier that day, the Dutch commander had said to them, 'You're safe,' and his stomach had knotted up with fear. He and Ines had looked at each other. 'Babo! Babo!' shouted Sead and pulled his hand; Safet was sleeping in Ines's arms. 'So we can go now,' the commander added and they left with a poor attempt at orderliness. He saw the frantic relief on their faces as they jumped into the transporters. At that moment, he realized how naively Bosniacs believed in Europe; they used to believe in Yugoslavia and when it started killing them off, they shifted their faith to Europe. But the Union was nothing but a business union and everything else was just a trinket, from culture to army. His country's market wasn't big enough to fight for; the good consumers had moved away and Europe had gladly taken them in. Later, when the Netherlands offered him asylum, he turned them down. I spit on them, he thought, and accepted Germany instead, though he was well aware that his parents' generation had spat on the Germans after the Second World War.) I mustn't move, somebody has descended into the pit, he's walking, bodies are shaking like planks, he's ransacking, looting, but they have already taken everything, they made us empty our pockets. It's hot, new flies are coming, the looter won't stop, he's ransacking, cursing, maybe he's one of those weekend soldiers you hear about, they work as officials or traders or whatever, living in Serbia and fighting in Bosnia on the weekends, coming with their caravans so they can load the loot and then going back to their offices on Monday mornings (this is just another trade, only they are dealing with Kalashnikovs, not contracts). Somebody shouts something at the one walking around the pit, he's very close and cursing more and more, there's nothing left, we've cleaned them out, the other one is shouting from the edge, the looter curses and clambers out, I mustn't move, the heat, the sun, can they see my stomach? Can I breathe? I can't feel my legs, I'm covered, pulsating pain in my left arm, flies. Flies. Buzzing, layers, covers of buzzing. I mustn't move. (When they raised their weapons, he had stepped before Ines and the children, grabbed Sead's head with his right hand and pushed the boy's face against his trouser leg. 'Close your eyes, son,' he said and then they started shooting. When he came to, flies, flies, flies everywhere.)

I mustn't move.

He opened his eyes and got lost in the whiteness of the wall. Flies were crawling all over him.

I mustn't move.

He looked down and saw the little German playing with her Barbie dolls. Why am I here? Why?

He heard somebody shout from the pit: 'Kill me!' and then gun shots. Why did he remain quiet?

Grette was combing a black-haired Barbie. 'Wie groß bist du geworden! Mashallah,' she added and knocked three times with her forefinger against the parquet floor.

Mashallah? But this wasn't her word; it was his word, his sons' word. He hadn't used it since their death. It meant 'God's will' – an expression you used after praising someone, followed by knocking on wood so nothing bad would happen to them. Where had Grette heard it? The kindergarten – there were a lot of Turks in her class. This word belonged to them and they had left it behind in Bosnia. And now here it was, in the middle of Berlin having reached this little German girl in a roundabout way – this word that his parents had passed down to him and he had passed down twice, in vain and never wanted to pass down again – it had followed him.

His skin was crawling with flies. He slowly got up, put down the potato, went over to his daughter and knelt down before her. She stopped playing and looked at him with wide eyes, holding the Barbie close to her chest. Flies swarmed over his arms as he opened them. Their tiny legs crawled over his palms.

Grette examined his arms and even leaned forward to see better.

He gazed at the top of her still head.

In a single move she swept her Barbie's hair over his palms. The flies drew back and hovered in the air a moment before settling back on his skin.

Grette lifted the doll toward his face. He lifted his right hand and let it barely touch the Barbie's arm, prickled by the sweaty warmness that comes from being gathered in a child's hands.

Lowering the Barbie, Grette pressed her face against his palm. Her whole body followed and his hand gave way as the little girl folded into his arms.

At first, he felt nothing. Then, in the moment her head settled against his chest, the flies became still.

Paul O'Reilly

Paul O'Reilly lives with his wife and children in Enniscorthy, County Wexford, Ireland. A recorded singer, songwriter and musician, Paul has performed on national radio and TV and with the Irish Chamber Orchestra. His drama has been shortlisted at *Listowel Writers' Week*, his fiction shortlisted for the *Seán O'Faoláin Prize* and selected for *The Lonely Voice* series of readings at the Irish Writers' Centre. Last March, Paul was first published in Irish Independent's *New Irish Writing*, edited by Ciaran Carty. He is currently shortlisted for the 2011 Hennessy Literary Awards.

What's Eating Him?

It was a hot Sunday, real hot, the kind of day when you just feel like lying in the shade. Her kid was skipping on the sidewalk outside the diner, say twelve, thirteen years old. She had on a flowered dress and was real steady, sounded like the rope was ticking. There weren't many cars about, only one other parked on the street. I walked up to her kid and stood and watched and she never once glanced at me, or broke her rhythm.

'It's a hot day for that,' I said, but her kid just stared right ahead.

I pulled open the screen door and stepped in and even though there were fans humming it was like the air had been baking in there for hours. Laura was listening to a fat guy, taking down his order. He was sitting at the counter, his Hawaiian shirt stretched to the limit, rising up his back, his trousers too small for him. I sat in the cubicle next to the door.

Laura said, 'Okay,' to the fat guy and stepped into the kitchen. When she came out, she came over and stood, her pencil ready, her hair tied back in a pony tail, the roots dark and shiny and said, 'Now, what can I get ya?'

I read the menu like I was hungry, then looked up and asked her the specials. As she rattled them off she was looking outside, the rope ticking behind me. She was slim for a woman who worked in a diner and her skin was clear.

'Hot today?' I said.

'Sure is,' she said.

'Your air-con broke?'

'Been broke as long as I've worked here.'

'I bet the kitchen's hot as hell.'

She smiled, said again, 'Sure is.'

'Just a Coke,' I said, leaving the menu back in the holder.

Walking to the counter her light, knee-length dress waved from side to side and it was the kind of dress that if she did a twirl it might rise up so you could see everything. When she stepped into the kitchen I moved to the counter where I could see right down along inside and took a seat on the opposite end to the fat guy who was still reading the menu, his elbows leaning either side. I could hear him breathing when he wasn't slurping his ice-water, that and the humming and the ticking of the rope. Laura came out with a glass full of ice, went to the fridge and grabbed my can. She had to lean down to get it and when her dress raised a little I just couldn't take my eyes off her. She brought the glass and can over, left them in front of me and when she cracked open the can the gassy sound made the fat guy look up. Some Coke fizzed up and out. Then she poured, watching it, me watching her.

'She's good on that rope,' I said. Laura smiled again and glanced at me, holding my stare for a second and that was good. 'She on some team?' I asked.

'Yeah,' Laura said, watching the Coke again.

'Helps keep her in shape then?'

'She's trying to make the basketball team in school. Coach has her eating all the right things, doing all this stretching in the mornings. Drives me crazy sometimes, trying to make her lunch.'

'But you work in a diner.'

'I know,' she said, raising an eyebrow.

'She's a good kid then.'

'Yeah,' she is.

Laura turned and stepped into the kitchen and the fat guy went back to reading the menu, the glass never far from his mouth. It wasn't long before Laura came out carrying a plate heaped with salad, looked like there was no meat on it from where I sat and she left it in front of the fat guy. He stared at the salad, like it was the wrong order, but then dowsed it with salt and pepper and some mayo. Laura watched him a few seconds and then rinsed a cloth and started wiping down the counter, her pony-tail swinging from side to side, she rising on her toes and reaching over to give the far side a rub. As she came closer I tried to stop staring and when I lifted my glass and can she said, 'Thanks,' and wiped away the rings.

'I was in last week,' I said. 'Last Sunday.'

'Yeah?'

'It was raining then, but you were working. It was busier.'

'Yeah, I was here last Sunday.'

'You work here every Sunday?'

She raised her eyebrow again, said, 'Yeah, most.'

'You must see a lot of faces then, hard to remember them all.'

'Yeah, it's hard to remember them all.'

'Some are easier to forget, I guess?'

'Not all,' she said, 'some are hard to forget, even if you want to.'

Her head tilted back a little as she smiled and she shifted her eyes to the side, like she was trying to see if the fat guy was watching.

I smiled then too and tipping my glass to her said, 'Fancy a Coke?'

'I never drink on duty,' she said.

'Maybe later then.'

She hesitated on this, then said, 'You're not from around, are you?'

'No.'

'You planning on hanging around?'

'Maybe.'

She rinsed the cloth again and stepped back into the kitchen. She stayed in there a while and in that time I sensed the fat guy staring at me, his plate clean and after wiping his mouth on the back of his hand and his forehead in a napkin he said in a fairly high pitched voice, 'You.'

'Excuse me,' I said.

'You,' he said again.

'Me?'

'She's taken.'

'Sorry?' I said.

He wiped his forehead again, said, 'That's her kid and she's not for the likes of you.'

'Say again,' I said.

He stood down off his stool, but was no taller for it, if anything he'd lost a couple of inches. He rooted in his pockets and threw some dollars on the counter, saying, 'You're not from around, you don't know anyone here.' Then he took a deep breath and winced like he had heartburn or something and said again, 'She's not for the likes of you. If I were you, I'd go.'

'What do you mean,' I said, 'the likes of me? What are you talking about?'

But he didn't answer, just dropped his head and turned and made for the door and when Laura came out she called after him, 'Jim, you haven't paid.'

But he didn't answer her either, just let the screen door slap closed and once outside he stood by her kid and starting talking to her, pointing inside. I could just about hear his voice over the humming and the ticking, but I couldn't make out the words.

'It's on the counter,' I said.

'What's eating him?' Laura asked and I could tell she'd fixed her hair and wiped her face. I even got a smell of soap.

'I don't know,' I said.

'He never leaves money on the counter,' she said, taking it up. Did he say anything?'

'Just that's your kid outside.'

'Oh, right. But you knew that already.'

'Yeah, she was here last Sunday too. She was serving then.'

When Laura looked outside so did I. Her kid was still skipping, the rope still ticking, though it seemed to be slowing down. 'I can't hear what Jim's saying to her.' Laura said then.

'Hardly giving her advice about her diet.'

'Well, our Jim wouldn't be one to give advice on anything.'

'You know him well?'

'Only all my life.'

She stepped to the fridge, opened the door, leaned down and she seemed to stay there longer than she needed to. Her legs were white, smooth and when she straightened she cracked open a can of Coke, licked away the fizz and took a sip. After licking her lips, she said, 'He's still there.'

I didn't look out at the fat guy this time, but did wonder what he'd meant when he said the likes of me. I wasn't from around here, sure and maybe she'd been brought up different to me, but I liked that in her and I liked the way she looked and how she moved. I liked the way she talked to strangers, the way she smiled, the way she talked about her kid.

'He said you were taken,' I said to her.

'What?' she said, resting the can against her shoulder.

'He said that, that you were taken.'

I couldn't tell if she was blushing or not, but it seemed she was waiting for me to carry on. 'Right,' she said then. 'And what if I wasn't?'

'Well, that would be better.'

'Why did you stop here?'

'I was passing by and was thirsty.'

'You've hardly touched it. Where you heading?'

'Little Rock.'

'Little Rock? That's a distance.'

'I like driving.'

'You drive a truck?'

I shook my head and said, 'Car.'

'Car? So what's a guy driving a car to Little Rock doing stopping here?'

'Well, I guess that depends on where you're driving from, don't it?'

'And you came by here last Sunday?'

'Yep.'

'That sounds like a lot of driving for someone that don't drive a truck.'

'Well, there's some nice scenery out here and I ain't never seen it before. So I thought I'd make a trip out, you know. I have some family settled close by now and they said that the drive was nice, that I'd like it.'

When Laura took a sip then so did I. 'Family,' she said, 'what kind of family?'

'The sister and brother-in-law kind.'

'And you're interested in scenery? You don't look like someone too interested in scenery to me.'

I took another sip and then said, 'Okay, well maybe I'm just interested in you then. How does that sound?'

Laura looked at me for a while and I was determined not to break her stare. Eventually she smiled and said, 'That sounds okay.'

'Okay then,' I said, extending my hand. 'My name is Earl.'

Laura took my hand, said, 'Nice to meet you, Earl. I'm Laura.'

'Nice to meet you, Laura,' I said and it was only when she looked outside that I noticed the ticking had stopped. Her kid was handing the fat guy the rope, the fat guy giving her dollars in return. Then her kid pointed down the street and the fat guy walked away in that direction with the rope. Then her kid came inside, staring at me the whole time she walked up to the counter where she sat up on the fat guy's stool.

'What did Jim say to you, honey?' Laura asked.

'Nothing, Mama,' her kid said, still staring at me, her eyes brown like her mother's. 'Can I have something to eat now, Mama?'

'Sure, honey,' Laura said. 'Honey, this is Earl, Earl this is my daughter, Meadow.'

'Nice to meet you, Meadow,' I saluted.

But Meadow said nothing, just carried on staring.

'What would you like, honey?' Laura asked.

'A cheeseburger with fries please, Mama.'

'A cheeseburger? But what about your diet, honey? What Coach was saying?'

'It's okay on Sundays, Mama. Coach says I can have a day off. That I can treat myself.'

'Oh,' Laura said, like it was news to her. 'Well, if Coach says so then I guess it's okay.' Laura glanced a smile at me and then stepped into kitchen and for the first time I could hear her talking with someone in there. Sounded like another woman.

'You're good on that rope,' I said. 'What position do you play?'

'You're not from around here, are you?' Meadow asked straight out.

'Now why is that of so much interest to people round here?'

'Are you divorced? You've no ring so you must be divorced.'

'I ain't never married,' I said, being honest with her, still hoping to get off on the right footing.

'My Mama is married,' Meadow started, 'and Papa says he'll never divorce her. He says he'll kill her before he divorces her. I stay with him Wednesday and Saturday nights and I tell him everything. That way he can keep an eye on Mama. And even though she says she'll never get back with him I know she will in the end. And Papa says so too.'

I wasn't sure what to say to that at first, but then decided to keep it honest and said, 'Your Papa sounds like a determined sort of man.'

'He is,' Meadow said and then a phone rang out back and we didn't talk as it rang, just waited till someone answered it.

'And what about your Mama then?' I asked. 'What has she to say about all this?'

'All what?'

'About her getting back with your Papa, when it seems clear to me she's no intention of doing any such thing.'

Meadow smiled for the first time, said, 'Papa says she ain't got no say in the matter. So there ain't nothing left to say about it.'

'I see,' I said 'and I guess it was around this time that maybe I started thinking she was telling the truth. Who was the guy you were talking to outside?' I asked.

'That's Uncle Jim.'

'And what about Uncle Jim then, he ain't going to do nothing stupid when I go outside now, is he?'

'Uncle Jim won't do nothing unless we say so. He ain't really with it, you see. That's the third time I've sold him that rope.'

'The third time?'

'Yeah, but still he can't lose no weight. Mama gives him salads everyday but he'll just go round Papa's later and Papa'll make him as many pancakes as he can eat. And then sometimes they drink and then they might go shooting down by the creek.'

'Your Uncle Jim owns a gun, does he?'

'No. Papa lets him borrow one of his. Papa has lots of guns and he gives me lessons too every Saturday. We start off down by the creek and shoot whatever moves. Then we move east looking for game. We like doing that together.'

'Shooting whatever moves?'

'We get quail, grouse and squirrels, sometimes pheasants. We shoot big game too. I've seen Papa get bear and deer. And Uncle Jim is strong so he helps Papa move it.'

'Your Mama know you do all this with your Papa and Uncle Jim?'

'No. That's between me and Papa and Uncle Jim. Mama's only interested in me playing basketball and I do that for her. She likes to come see me play.'

'That's mighty nice of you,' I said and then Meadow smiled again, but this one was the kind of smile that was hard to make out, if it was real or put on.

I excused myself and in the washroom I stood by the urinal for surely five minutes but nothing came. I buttoned up then and washed my hands and cupped water and soaked my face and in the mirror I watched the water run and drop off my chin down the drain, still trying to figure her out. Then I dried myself in a paper towel and balled it up and dropped it in the basket.

On my way out I overheard Laura talking to Meadow about Uncle Jim and how often he calls, 'And you know he calls in the middle of the night, honey, she said, you've heard it yourself. And he calls a few times if he's been drinking. You know I do wish he wouldn't drink so much. It's not good for him.'

When she saw me she asked, 'Everything alright in there, Earl?'

'Sure,' I said, 'though I think I'll be hitting the road now, Laura. The day ain't getting any longer sitting here.'

'But you haven't finished your Coke,' Laura said and then she looked to Meadow.

'That's alright,' I said, hitching up my belt and heading for the counter. 'I don't think it was agreeing with me to be honest about it, ladies.'

I threw down some dollars but Laura didn't move to take them. I saluted her then and said, 'See you round,' but she didn't answer me. I saluted Meadow too but she made no reaction either and it was only as I pushed open the screen door Laura asked Meadow, 'Did you say something to him?'

'No, Mama,' Meadow said, all innocent like and I almost believed her myself.

Outside I walked to my car pretty fast, listening for a door opening, footsteps other than mine, something, but heard nothing only the hum of traffic from the highway nearby. The handle of the car almost burned and even after leaving the windows down, when I sat in I felt faint with the heat. I started the car, put up the windows, turned up the air-con and as I pulled and fastened my seatbelt I noticed the other car still on the street, facing me, Uncle Jim sitting in it, his window down, his elbow pointing out the window.

I wondered what he'd done with the rope and thought about what Meadow had said and then about turning round but my entry was beyond Uncle Jim's car. I hit the locks, revved the engine and tried to imagine the sound the wind would make once I gathered speed on the highway. Then I set off, slowly, just crawling along the sidewalk leading up to the diner, trying to pretend Uncle Jim wasn't there and that Meadow was still skipping on the sidewalk and that I'd never set foot in that diner and spotted Laura. But still I was too hot and thirsty to forget about her just like that, though I had a real bad feeling inside that this thirst I had was the kind that could really get someone hurt if I was none too careful, if I didn't soon hit that gas.

Nastasya Parker

Nastasya Parker grew up in New Hampshire, USA and now lives in Gloucestershire, England with her husband and son. This is her second story to be featured in a Bristol Short Story Prize Anthology. She received a degree in Writing and Literature a few years ago, a generally exciting endeavour which left her ill-prepared for her current, more tedious task of getting an NVQ in Health and Social Care. She works in a nursing home and as a waitress and should really crack on with her half-finished novel.

Cats and Elephants

Cindy sleeps as if she's trying to knock herself out. On her side, fist aimed at her chin, elbow trespassing onto my half of the bed. Her bottom pooched behind her as if she's already taken a blow to the stomach. We've lived together for months now but it still makes me wonder, What happens if the Cindy she's fighting beats the one lying next to me?

She sleeps like someone still young. I'm almost ten years younger but I've settled into nightly stomach-down slumber rather than sideways sprawl. If age were measured in peaceful nights, though, I suppose she'd be the younger one, after years of rising to tuck little ones back into bed.

'You were doing it again,' I tell her over instant coffee. We lean against the scarred kitchen counter, neglecting the chairs with torn vinyl cushions while our soggy bath towels languish over their backs. 'Boxing with yourself in your sleep.'

She chuckles. 'So that's why I feel beat up in the mornings. And I'd worried it was old age.'

'It's bad for your spinal curvature, lying on your side.' I stack our emptied Special K bowls in the sink. 'I've got to protect your curves for my own devious reasons.'

She fingers her damp hair. 'I'll do the dishes later, we'd better get going.'

Whenever I compliment her looks she changes the subject. I suppose if someone said that to me, I probably wouldn't respond with a breezy, 'Why, thank you.' Still I voice my appreciation. That must be one reason why Cindy stays.

I grab our lunchbags and shut the fridge door after three attempts. The lining is loose on the bottom of the door, so it doesn't stick well. Nothing's built to last in this flat. 'One day…' I could finish this sentence so many ways. One day we'll be a real couple, get our own furniture, maybe a pet. But best keep it light. I warn her, 'One day, we'll wake to find your elbow stuck in your ear. Or mine.'

'In your-rear?' She smiles as I lace my trainers.

'That might take some acrobatics.'

Cindy's told me how, when she was very small and she started going with her family to church, she used to sit colouring in an activity book while everyone stood up to sing hymns. She's described the voices swelling; she would lean against the pew and feel the wood vibrate in the vocal storm. And sometimes the words clouded together. 'May it be a sweet, sweeeeet sound in your rear.' Her Crayola lines would wobble as she tried not to laugh.

She assumed her family and even, later, her own children wouldn't appreciate this, so I was the first person she shared it with. While we were just friends, having coffee after work. She would have gotten up at five to prepare a casserole for her family in the slow-cooker and buy herself time for me. 'It's sad,' she'd remarked, 'when you can't tell the ones you love about the things that make you smile… or the people who do.'

Now, she never mentions The Ones She Loved to me. The love has transferred but brought taboos along with it. Must it be so?

She locks the door of the apartment. All three locks. She can't get enough of locking.

I follow her down trash-strewn stairs, skipping the tilty boards on the third and tenth steps. The sun glares, forcing our eyes from the rickety houses across the street, to the car park on our right. And beyond that, the currently impotent streetlights where the banner once hung across the road.

Come home, Mom! Does she hear them saying it in her head, even weeks after we finally convinced the town council to have the sign removed? Would I love her less if she never thought of them, or less if she always did?

That was only the start of the campaign. Her family, no doubt funded by their church, ran a couple of newspaper ads and the condemnation spread beyond personal ties and organisations. Today, the word HOMEWRECKER is spraypainted, black, on the side of my old Buick.

Nothing to be done about it now. I open my door and the letters HO spring forth. Witty. I toss my head to look at the windows of our building and the others around it. Who was it this time? Perhaps the solemn, bearded man who occasionally sits barefoot on cigarette-littered front steps, playing cello. Or the foul-mouthed parents of the tiny children who have nothing to do but play with a rusty hacksaw on the lawn. There are the teenagers who leave beer cans under the trees out back; the enormously fat couple always shouting at their dog. When we moved here we loved people-watching. But people aren't all they're cracked up to be.

Cindy locks the car doors once we're in. They never locked their house in the woods; her husband objected at having to rummage in the pockets of his flannel shirts for the key. Of course, he wouldn't eat steak unless it could be cut with the side of his fork. Couldn't be bothered lifting two pieces of silverware at once. Fortunately for the kids, he found time for the occasional ball game or model-building session. Unfortunately for Cindy, that means he commands their fierce loyalty.

'We could paint a mural over the car doors,' she says.

'Or classier still, get wood panelling down the sides.'

We're listening to the Eagles on the stereo. A song of lost love plays and I wince. I feel sorry for her husband sometimes. Surely rejection hurts even from someone you've barely noticed in years.

We work at the hospital; she was secretary for the on-site daycare when we met. Now she helps in various departments, so she's not locked into any one place. No one from outside can find her.

I'm still an assistant at the daycare. The new secretary is an older lady who looks over her glasses at everyone. When we've crossed paths in the hallway, alone, she seems alarmed, as if I am a secretary-predator. Not Cindy's lover. Today she tells me, 'Someone's here to see you. He's having coffee in the kitchenette.'

I head that way with trepidation. The gentleman caller is slight, wearing a dark green bomber jacket and his orange hair is slicked back. 'Ms Favrell. Good morning. You know who I am?'

He looks like a leprechaun; that's all I can come up with. 'Sorry, no.'

His smile tightens to a grimace. 'Right. That's probably because you haven't done any volunteering with us yet.' He strokes the handle of the flowery mug the secretary must have fixed him up with. 'Chris Mehrlin, president of the local chapter of GLAAD. We've been fighting to pass the Civil Partnerships Act for this state, so –you see why I'm here?'

'You visit everyone pursuing a gay relationship?'

He sighs. His words ooze, possibly the most repugnant rationality I've ever heard. 'It's essential to show our relationships are as moral as heterosexual ones. For you and Mrs Hurd to carry on in such a controversial way – well, you're giving the enemy ammunition.'

Condemnation really does spread. I fold my arms across my chest, suddenly cold. 'I didn't realise GLAAD had a moral police division.'

'It's not your relationship that makes us uneasy; it's the high profile of it.'

'High profile? Our idea of a night out is a walk by the river and toasties from a gas station!'

He's a foot shorter than I am, but he cocks his head so somehow he's looking down at me. His eyes are serious and as unfeeling as those of a presidential silhouette on a coin. 'You're jeopardising the happiness and stability of many people just like you.'

I straighten. 'I'm not about advancement, just love. You're elevating a cause above individuals and I think you'll find 'the enemy' – I indicate quotation marks; it sure as hell isn't my term – 'does that too.' How else do you explain Cindy's family and church beseeching her through the paper to come home, but never answering her phone calls or letters? I wonder at this for the millionth time as I sweep through the swinging door of the kitchenette.

One child was withdrawn from our daycare since the news about Cindy and me and a couple of parents made idle threats. Always with the excuse that, 'We'd react this way if you were straight, too.' But the hospital has been supportive. We're not hurting anybody, not there at least.

Kids still pounce on me when I enter, the littlest waving a copy of The Gruffalo. 'Do the voices!' he pleads, pulling his thumb from his mouth.

'Can we have a treasure hunt today?'

'First come to our restaurant,' commands a girl in a chef's hat, indicating the play kitchen in the corner.

'Well,' I answer, 'before I sample your restaurant menu, I'll need some money. So I'll go treasure hunting. And to treasure hunt like a proper pirate...' I scoop up The Gruffalo holder as his lip starts to tremble '...I'll need a parrot on my shoulder. That means you'll help with the funny voices!'

The other playleaders have little ones at home, so they're often too tired for such things. But for my affections, these kids have no competition; they can be themselves. That was why Cindy took interest in me. Strange, it enticed her to leave her husband and somehow estrange her own six kids. In winning her over, have I risked destroying the person who was initially attracted to me?

As we begin our hunt, we encounter a gathering at the back entrance. Little Nora is showing off one of her cat's eight-week-old kittens. 'We have a black one, three stripy ones and a grey one,' she announces. 'Their eyes are open now, look!'

'Careful, Nora.' Her mother sways the kitten, cupped in her hands, away from thrusting fingers.

This is a stripy one, with white feet, a particularly pink nose and green eyes wide-open indeed. 'Are they – ' I want to ask when they can leave their mother. But those words are awkward for me, so these happen to come out instead: 'Can I have one?'

My surprise only lasts a moment; so does theirs. Nora's mother says, 'Want me to bring her back at going-home time?'

I told my parents months ago, over Sunday dinner. We'd always gotten along well, even living together as adults. With my brothers not in touch unless they needed money, I figured I couldn't go awfully wrong. 'You two are finally getting rid of me. Cindy and I found a place together.'

My father chewed his roast beef thoughtfully.

'Oh, we'll miss you, honey,' Mom gushed, 'but I'm glad you've got a good friend like her.'

'She is a good friend. We also happen to be in love.'

Mom made to stand up. 'You know, I think there are more mashed potatoes in the kitchen.'

Dad put his hand on hers. 'Calm down. Let's talk about this. Amy?' He looked at me.

'I'm gay.' Or did that only apply to men? I hadn't done research; I just knew my feelings. 'Um, I'm a lesbian.'

My father chewed more thoughtfully, his Adam's apple bobbing over the collar of his flannel shirt as if it was at sea.

'How about a cat?' Mom chirped. 'Remember, you always wanted a cat! We could choose one together; I'm sure I'd manage my allergies...'

And now I have a cat and Cindy. Something more to hold. An extra source of warmth. Someone else on my side, for Cindy to consider when she wrestles with herself. After work I wait in the car park for her to finish. I sit on the Buick driver seat, cradling the kitten, my legs outside the open door, disrupting the graffiti. Pet names cavort in my mind: Muriel, Honey, Aphrodite perhaps? Or Lilac, Cindy's favourite flower.

I tickle the kitten's belly. She bats my fingers, her eyes pupil-black and fierce.

'What – what did you do?' Cindy asks from around the open door.

'I got us a pet.'

She shakes her head, her eyes wide as the kittens'. The animal distresses her more than the black spraypainted HO. 'We can't take care of a cat.'

Says who? Her husband's church? The local newspaper, the moral police division of GLAAD? 'Come on! Aren't you tired of people telling us what we can't do? We have plenty of love to go around. And we'll keep it secret from the landlord. The apartment's such a wreck anyway, I don't know what he's trying to protect – ' When she doesn't speak, I stand and touch her arm. 'What's wrong? You like cats.'

She scurries away, crying for the first time since we moved in together.

I find her on the bench where I first saw her cry, when we were just friends. We'd been for a lunch-hour stroll and seen a lone, pink baby sock in the mud. 'That's what their childhoods are like,' she'd wept. 'You have something tiny and perfect, you're walking along through life and suddenly you realise it's gone.'

'So that's why you decided to have more and more kids?' I tried to be jovial.

'I didn't decide anything,' she mumbled. 'I just didn't decide to not have them. And then I spent every second on church, cooking, doing laundry, stopping the floorboards from crumbling beneath their feet... I don't think I've taken my youngest anywhere on her own, not even shopping. She just gets hand-me-downs.'

'So take her out!' I had urged. It seemed so obvious.

'She's thirteen. She wouldn't even want to now.'

I can't imagine Cindy's family mean to hurt or forget her. I can't imagine her being the useless mother she insists she was.

Now, I sit beside her, struggling to maintain my grasp on the little cat. I should know by now: the things you get excited to hold, don't stay still in your hands. It happens with people, pets – even causes. Perhaps this is the real reason Cindy fights in her sleep. 'Cin...'

She twists a sodden tissue in her lap. 'I always wondered why my parents gave me a name that could be shortened to sin. Maybe they were prophets.'

'What's so sinful about us living together and keeping a cat?'

'I couldn't keep my own kids,' she whimpers.

The kitten claws me; I kiss its head. 'We'll start over!'

Cindy stares. Okay, never imply to a mother that a cat can replace her six kids. It's like telling your daughter a cat will 'cure' her homosexuality.

'I mean...' The kitten purrs inexplicably. I go for broke. 'Listen, you're irresistible. Your kids aren't going to stay away. They're defensive now; it's like a war.' I think of Mr. Mehrlin's metaphors. 'When the rhetoric subsides and they start feeling beyond anger, they'll want to see you.'

Cindy unlocks her grip on the hankie to caress the cat's paw. 'What about us?'

I'm surprised she's the one asking. It's the same question I asked when she first kissed me and I give her the answer she gave me. 'Well, I want you today and I'm pretty sure I'll want you tomorrow and probably the day after.'

She still looks sad, but she says, 'If they come see us, they'll like the cat.'

'Yeah, she'll break the ice.' I lay the kitten on Cindy's lap and she clings to it.

'Maybe we should do a little decorating too,' she suggests.

'Can't hurt.' We walk towards the car. 'I know, we'll name the cat Elephant. If we have a brand new Elephant in the room, it might help people forget the old one.'

She laughs. Teeth white, dimples buried in her cheeks like treasure that laid hidden for decades.

Robert Perry

Rob Perry was born and raised in Norfolk but doesn't have a regional accent and is soon to graduate from the University of East Anglia's Creative Writing programme. Typically a short story writer, he occasionally flirts with novels and longer works. He is banned from Waterstone's. This is his first published work.

Open Mike Night

A poem regarding my love for Amander

Her name is Amander. I am confident that my poetry will make her want to be my girlfriend. It is open mike night and although I am wearing my best jeans, they are tight and I am forced to frequently adjust them. It is a Tuesday.

I am sitting in the village hall and tonight it is full of old people. They temporarily fill chairs and prepare themselves for my masterwork. I say hello to Susan and Trevor from next door, even though they both smell of beige and I take a seat at the back. I listen to their poetry; it is about withering trees and winter. This means they expect to die soon.

Amander arrives late. She is wearing a tracksuit and has thickly applied make-up on her face. She is beautiful. I do not love her purely for her aesthetic qualities though. She is with her friends and laughing like we will laugh when we are married.

After around 20 minutes my name is called out.

'Mike, are you ready to read your poem?' asks Judy, the vicar's wife. I stand up and nod confidently. Amander appears to notice my confidence. She is looking at me now, so I wink at her. I ask her to come to the front.

'Amander, would you come to the front?' I say. She looks at me blankly and then back towards her friends. They nudge her forwards, clearly aware that destiny cannot be ignored. She has a look that says 'I can't believe this is happening.' I tell her this is really happening.

'Amander' I say, 'This is really happening.' I hand her the red T-shirt I have with me for the finale and she holds it. She obviously does not want to sully this pristine moment by wearing the T-shirt.

I walk to the podium and open up my Microsoft PowerPoint presentation on the whiteboard. On it I have all the pictures I found on her work website and 'Myspace' profile. I have enabled PowerPoint's scrolling function so that they will alternate while I read. The title page is a photo-edited picture of the two of us. The pictures that follow are a combination of her at work and her in more relaxed, social environments. They alternate. I had considered a drum, to punctuate my love for her, but had left late and could not securely fasten it to my Raleigh race bike. I told the audience this and that they should take it into consideration.

I begin.

A is for Amazing. The room is now silent, everyone looking directly at me, the occasional glance toward Amander. They must be hypothesising about how ridiculously happy she currently is.

M is for Monday. The day you put your washing out. I know this because I overheard you saying so, not because I have been to your house.

Snippets of conversation begin to breakout but I know they are admiring words, so I smile knowingly and continue.

A is for accessible. I feel we are suitably matched, both physically and emotionally.

A rush of excitement as Amander sneezes. It is the second most attractive thing she has ever done in my presence. Once she threw a disposable coffee cup in a bin near my seat. I kept it.

N is the 14th letter of the English alphabet, a consonant. We both use the alphabet in day-to-day interactions.

D is for door. Your door is green. I have to walk past it on my way to Tesco. Although their prices are marginally more expensive than my more local Morrisons branch, I feel their produce is of a higher general standard. I do not mind paying slightly more for this.

The room is as I imagined, their faces are in awe. Perhaps some of them realise that this is the defining moment in a lasting and meaningful modern day love story.

E is for Euthanasia. If you died, I would travel to Sweden to do this.

R is for red. She is still holding the red T-shirt. I repeat this line to make it more poignant and begin singing the first lines of 'Lady in Red' by Chris de Burgh. By now she is so in love with me she cannot look me in the eye. She is laughing with joy. I move in closer and kiss her forehead. She cannot believe I have done this.

Now is the time. I drop onto my knee 'Amander' I proclaim, 'be my life partner!'

Upon doing this, I tear open my neatly pressed shirt with a complete disregard for the needle time sewing the buttons back on will necessitate and reveal to her, in all its glory, the T-shirt I made for her on the internet.

I LOVE AMANDER FOREVER. It says.

She tells me I have spelt her name incorrectly.

Philip St John

Philip St John's short stories have been published in *New Irish Writing*, broadcast on RTE radio and nominated for a Hennessy Literary Award. Like *The Last Fare*, his first novel *Crazy Baldheads* is set in the Caribbean – Philip taught for a couple of years in Jamaica. His first play, *Maxine*, which is also set in the Caribbean, won an award from the International Playwrights' Forum and received a rehearsed reading in Germany in June 2011. In 2010 he received a Literary Bursary from The Arts Council Of Ireland for his novel-in-progress, which is not set in the Caribbean. He is also working on a play and short stories.

The Last Fare

It is late when the young white couple emerge from the terminal. Dudley watches them approach the first cab in the line, both in short sleeves, the man pushing a luggage trolley. The woman leans down to speak through the driver's window. She doesn't have to lean down very far: she is small, a plump blonde. Even five cars away, leaning against the door of his Sierra, Dudley can see how tired her smile is. She gives the same smile at the window of the second car and the third. Dudley can hear her voice now. Though the last flight came from Miami, she doesn't sound American. English, maybe.

The sky flickers, a branch of lightning over the silhouetted city. The road and footpath are wet. Brown water stands in the potholes. Dudley lights up his half-smoked cigar. The couple are trying the fourth cab now. The driver shakes his head and the couple turn towards Dudley, the woman smiling at him. He notices the make up around her eyes is a little smudged. Perhaps she was crying on the plane. Probably they are late for some important event – Dudley has worked the airport route for more than twenty years and knows the stories. This one will end with him being asked to go somewhere inconvenient and dangerous. It's a long time since he has seen so many taxi men refuse a fare.

There are no more cars after Dudley's, but that won't stop him refusing the couple. It does not matter what they offer. He may even quit for the night now. In a few minutes he could be home, tiptoeing into the darkness of the room he shares with Precious and the baby. Often it takes him an hour or two to slip into sleep. In the next room, Mrs Williams, the fat teacher who has sub-let to him and Precious and four other couples, will be shifting around in her bed, or kissing the man she has in sometimes. Dudley has never heard such a noisy kisser. It sounds like she is wetly smacking her man.

'Chapeltown, yuh say?' Dudley blows out smoke and glances over the woman's head at the young man behind the trolley. He is tall, with broad shoulders. His blank expression may hide impatience or contempt.

'No miss. Sorry nuh. Wait til daylight. Taxi tek yuh den.'

The couple keep staring, as if his words are still travelling towards them, slowed by the humidity, which has risen since the last shower.

'We'll give you...' The woman glances up at the man.

'A hundred.'

Dudley chuckles.

'Oh come on.' The woman's smile is teasing. Her weepy make-up gives her a slightly crazed air. 'A hundred dollars for a fifty mile drive.'

'Road not safe.' Dudley stretches. 'Wait til mornin.'

'A hundred and fifty,' the man says.

Chuckling, stretching, Dudley walks off along the footpath. He dozed through most of the last downpour. He is groggy and stiff. Over the flat roof of the building comes the powerful whine of a jet engine. Ahead of him is the mesh fence of the car-rental lot. The couple could rent a car. But it would be murder to suggest that. At least he knows the roads and the signs of trouble. He turns: they are still by his taxi, talking. The man pulls a wallet from his pocket. Dudley wants to turn away. Let them offer someone else two hundred, or two fifty. Then he won't have to turn it down.

'My sister is the bride, Ciara.' The woman speaks to Dudley over his left shoulder. Aoife is her name. Delighted that she can smoke in the car, she has lit up three cigarettes in a row. In the rear view mirror, Dudley can see her husband, Tadgh. He is in the corner of the back seat, sulkily gazing at the tin-roofed shacks along the edge of the highway. Sometimes tourists ask Dudley to stop here and he photographs them against a backdrop of mothers in singlets holding babies, barbed wire, colourful graffiti, a plane lifting into the sky. 'She loves the island. Came on holiday a few years back. Hasn't talked about anything else since. So when her boyfriend dropped on one knee, she said, "Well all right, if we can have it in Chapeltown."'

A strange monster of an insect hits the windscreen. It's right in front of him, a desperate buzz of wings, a dark hole of open mouth, expressionless eyes. Suddenly the creature is gone. Aoife continues to talk, pulling on her cigarette. 'Do you know 'The Right Place' at all, Dudley?'

There's a faint smell of alcohol on her breath. She's not drunk. She must have had a couple of drinks on the plane, or in Miami during the delay. He tries to picture where she lives. It is often a surprise to discover the kinds of homes visitors have. He has driven tourists around for a whole day and they seem like carefree kids. Then they show him pictures on their phone. Two of them – living in a place that big! Often in the pictures the couples look older. They wear heavier, more formal clothes. That's when he realises he does not know these people. If he took up their invitations to America and England, they probably would not recognise him.

'The Right Place. Yeah, I heard of it, mon. Tell me more.'

'Well, it's a holiday village near Chapeltown with, you know, the usual – the pools and the apartments, the cafes and restaurants, a theatre and nightclub. But it's run on a principle of fairness.' The young woman sounds grave. He can see her pale face in the mirror. She is looking into his eyes. 'Everyone is paid properly. The food is locally sourced. Profits are spent in the area and the village supports local schools and medical centres. Great, isn't it?'

Dudley nods and fights off a yawn. He is fifty-three now and the interrupted sleep he grabs during daytime rarely refreshes him. He thinks about Mrs Williams, the smacking noises of her kisses in the next room. He thinks about Raphael and Horace, the sons of another tenant, Gladys. They are lively boys and Gladys cannot control them. This afternoon, when they came home from school they caused a commotion. He remembers rushing blearily into the next room, a kitchen, where Georgina, the four-year-old child of another tenant was screaming. Raphael and Horace had been collecting cockroaches in a bucket for days. They had thrown the contents on the little girl as she sat reading a picture book.

He drives along the road through the cane fields. There is no light apart from the beams of his headlamps. The left beam skews off into the verge. Maybe he will get that fixed with the money from this job. He listens to the music pouring from the speakers at the back of the car. Classical. He doesn't know the composer's name. Some tourist left behind a heap of cassette tapes years ago. Lots of passengers ask why he does not play reggae. Dudley never answers that. Tourists don't want a taxi driver complaining about the country in which they have come for a holiday. In response, he'll put on a reggae station and the tourists will sing along with Marley, Gregory Isaac, Black Uhuru. They often know all the words. Can even tell him what 'uhuru' means. Freedom.

After it leaves the dark sea of cane, the road narrows, a ribbon winding into hills thick with woods. This is a popular place with tourists in daytime and you have to drive slowly then as you are sure to encounter minibuses, rented cars and taxis parked around a bend, visitors standing on a precipice, water sparking down a gorge behind them. Or they might be filming across a valley of ferns, or photographing the faded colours of wooden homes in a village way up on one of the peaks. He likes driving people up here in daytime. The beauty of the land helps him to recall why he chose to stay on the island as a youth. His brother Isaac moved to Canada the year he left school. He started a business there and asked Dudley to come and help. Now Isaac has three restaurants. He is very busy and since their mother died, only comes home on business. He stays in a hotel and meets his food suppliers there. Dudley meets him there too. Dressed in a shirt and tie, he sits with his brother in the hotel's air-conditioned restaurant. The menus are sizeable and bound in leather.

He lowers the volume of the music on the climb into the hills. The girl has fallen quiet. She may be asleep. Her husband is definitely sleeping, his head swaying each time the car rounds a bend. Dudley is aware of the anxious beating of his heart. He is conscious of the dark woods on either side, his distance from the populous lowlands.

The headlights sweep across columns of tree trunks. Then swing back the other way. And back again. A noise from behind startles him. A click, accompanied by a flash in the rear-view mirror. The young woman lighting another cigarette.

'God, I need a bed. I'll shove Ciara out of hers if that's what it takes.'

Dudley grins. 'Want me to change the music?'

It is a sad passage, slow and heavy.

'Not at all. Listen away. Who is it? Mozart or somebody? I'm useless with classical. Good, isn't it?'

Dudley nods. He's not sure why, because he has just noticed faces – in the trees, ducking behind a trunk as a headlight hits them. He brakes, hard. 'Jesus!' The girl has slammed against the back of his seat. Dudley wrestles with the gear stick. The car is almost twenty years old. It is always a struggle to get into reverse. He knows he will succeed if he relaxes, concentrates. The girl's cigarette has fallen on his thigh, burning a dark patch there. He is conscious of a sharp pain like a pin-prick as he brushes it off. And he is into reverse, his head turned as he speeds back towards the bend. But something is already there, blocking the road, the limb of a tree, figures standing around it. 'Get down! Down – get down!' he shouts and bends low as he forces the gears into first and lurches back uphill, knowing there will be another roadblock around the bend.

'Oh God… God!' This is Aoife. Dudley can feel her tremble. The shivering travels through the materials of the car. He has stopped and turned off the engine. Three men with torches and machine guns are approaching from the roadblock ahead.

'It's okay, honey. It's all right.' The young man Tadgh stares at him, questioningly, in the rear view mirror. Dudley thinks about a run into the trees. If each of them rushes out a different door, it will confuse the bandits. One or two or all three of them might escape. But the couple aren't alert enough. They aren't really here yet. They are still on the plane, or in Ireland.

'Listen to me!' He turns and grabs her arm, hard. 'Both of you – listen. Do what they say. Exactly. And be polite,' he adds to Tadgh.

He pushes open his door and steps out with his hands raised. So does Tadgh, who spends a few moments persuading the girl to follow him.

'Take what you want.' Tadgh squints into the light of a torch. He is standing tall, looking authoritative. Dudley imagines him in an office, talking to an employee. Both of them wearing suits. High up in a building overlooking a city.

The bandits have scarves over their faces, like the bad men in a cowboy film. Their eyes look wild. One man looks wilder than the rest. He is taller and moves in a strange, jerky way. Over his T-shirt he wears a sleeveless padded jacket with many pockets. A weapon protrudes from each pocket. Dudley sees knives, lengths of metal with sharpened points, a revolver, hatchets, hammers. No wonder the man is breathing hard.

The smallest of the men is their leader. Torchlight shows some patches of grey in his hair. His eyes are not quite as wild as the others'. They gleam with faint amusement.

'Tank you,' he says to Tadgh and nods at the third man to open the boot. Two others are coming up the road. These are the men Dudley saw first, in the trees. One of them stops on the bend, looking downhill. The other helps with the emptying of the boot.

'Hey!'

Tadgh steps towards Crazy Man, who is fingering the thin gold chain around Aoife's throat. One of the men at the boot turns. He puts the barrel of his machine gun against Tadgh's head. He is as tall as

Tadgh and wears no shoes. His open shirt is grimy and his trousers end raggedly at his knees. Maybe the bandits live rough in the hills. There are old settlements where runaway slaves once hid together. Perhaps that is where they live, a place hard to find and attack.

They open the suitcases and begin to transfer the contents into black plastic bags: clothes, cosmetics, shoe polish, paperbacks, a radio, soap, a box of tea, a gift-wrapped box. Everything is of interest, apparently.

The leader tells the girl to remove her jewellery. She does, her hands trembling, Tadgh's arm around her shoulder.

Sometimes people survive an ambush. So Dudley has heard from other taxi men. He trusts the leader of this gang. He is slower, more thoughtful than his underlings.

Tadgh and Aoife hand over their shoes. A man searches inside the car. He leaves the tapes on the floor, but tears off the air-freshener that dangles from the mirror. Dudley feels a dull annoyance at that. Air-freshener. Mon. But he keeps his anger to himself. Rely on the leader. He will spare them. He is a clever, resourceful man. In another life, he would be as successful as Dudley's brother, or Tadgh.

'Bloodclaat!'

This is Crazy Man. He stoops to the ground, fumbling for a strip of cloth. The weapons and tools in his pockets shake around. Dudley glares at the couple. But they don't seem to notice. Dumbly they gape at the exposed face of Crazy Man. It is a distinctive face, long, with huge upper teeth and a dark scar along the chin. Crazy Man pushes the cloth over his mouth. But he has to remove it again while he puts his machine gun on the ground and then, with both hands free, ties the scarf behind his head.

'Bloodclaat…Bloodclaat!' Crazy Man mutters as his hands fumble with the knot. The other men are staring at the leader. They are holding the plastic bags of swag. Crazy Man looks at the leader too. For the first time their boss looks uncertain. His men wait.

He nods at the two bandits holding the bags. A slight nod, but sharp. He gestures his machine gun at the couple, then at the trees on the other side of the road. The ground falls away there, towards a valley.

'Go wit de men,' he says to Tadgh and Aoife.

The young white man stands tall. 'Why? Go where?'

The leader does not meet his gaze. 'Do wha yuh told, bwoy!'

Tadgh glances at Dudley and Dudley looks away. It is stupid to be vexed with the couple. They are young, inexperienced. And perhaps the leader intended to kill them all along. For some reason, he pictures his brother Isaac flirting with a waitress. Isaac is reading a wine list through fancy glasses. His teeth are very white. Then he imagines Precious, her round softness in the dark, the noises of the baby in the corner of the room. Never has Dudley felt such a rage to live. Never have things been so clear.

The couple and the two men with the bags fade into the trees. The leader and Crazy Man gesture Dudley towards the trees on the other side of the road. Why the separate groups? It would make bodies harder to find. Perhaps that is it.

Once he is a little distance into the wood, he will run. With the trees so close together, it is possible that he will evade the bullets. It will be dark in there too. But he knows that escape is unlikely. Rage has given him a sense of great energy, but these men are much younger than him. They know the area. He glances at the leader and sees the eyes above the scarf change expression. It might be sympathy, or regret. The expression passes quickly. Now his eyes show little character at all. It's not that they are cold. This is probably how Dudley looked, back at the airport when he negotiated with the Irish pair: professional.

Genevieve Scott

Genevieve Scott was born and lives in Toronto, Canada. By day she works as a communications professional at a children's hospital. In the evenings she writes and re-writes short stories at her kitchen table. In 2010 Genevieve won the *White Wall Review/G. Raymond Chang Prize for Creative Writing* (Toronto). Her work has appeared in the *White Wall Review* (Toronto) and the *Paragon Press* (St.John's, Newfoundland).

Ernie Breaks

At the end of every school year, Mom buys Jed and me a 'passing' present. This time I want her to get us a puppy.

'Out of the question, Cara,' Mom says, throwing a pack of birthday candles into the shopping cart. 'I don't want to be the one picking up dog crap for the next ten years. The way you and your brother are with toys, don't tell me it's not going to be like that. You loved your skateboards last summer, yesterday I practically broke my neck on one in the laundry room.'

'But it's different,' I tell her. 'A dog isn't a toy, it's a real live thing.'

Mom picks up an Angel Food cake, but I stop her before it goes into the cart. 'Devil's,' I say, pointing at the chocolate mixes on the higher shelf. I am hanging off the cart with my hands on the bar and my feet on the lower tray with her cans of tonic water. She drops the chocolate mix into the front basket and it makes me lose my balance.

'If you really want a pet, let's start with fish,' she says, pushing the cart forward. 'I know a guy from Quit4Life who may give us a deal.' I don't really want fish, but a deal always makes Mom in a better mood. Even though today's our passing party, Mom is still grouchy.

We drive to the fish place after the groceries. The store has a big tangle of plants in the window and it's dark and wet inside, like walking into someone's mouth. A man waves to us from the back of the store and smiles so big I can see the gold wrapped around his back teeth.

'Yoo hoo! What a surprise!' he says. He kisses Mom on the cheek.

'Isn't Gary's store neat?' Mom says, like I'm six years old. To Gary she says, 'We're looking for a passing present for Cara and her brother, Jed. Cara just finished grade four.'

Gary makes that frown face with high eyebrows that is supposed to mean he's impressed. Mom doesn't tell Gary that Mrs Ludy said my progress in math over the last year makes me a borderline candidate for the Special Ed room in September. Jed calls it the retard room.

Gary rubs his hands together. 'Very nice, little lady,' he says, 'very nice.' And then for no reason that I can tell, he says, 'Shall we go fishing then?' in an English accent.

He takes us over to a tank crammed with white fish that have black lines running through them like jail uniforms. 'Angelfish,' he says, drawing a line on the glass with his finger. 'Graceful, huh?'

'No, not *angel* fish,' I say. 'Jed won't like them. They sound gay.'

'Cara!' Mom says. Her neck turns the colour of a ham.

'Well, now,' Gary says, giggling. 'Let's not make references to people's sexual preferences.' He touches Mom's shoulder.

'What?' I say. I wonder if Gary has a crush on Mom.

'I'm sorry, Gary,' Mom says, 'I think we might have meant something different there.'

'That's alright, Lorna,' Gary says. 'We understand.' He wipes his fingers on his sweatpants and then smiles at me extra big. 'Have you ever thought about a turtle? Turtles can be a lot of fun.'

The turtles at the back of the store have red ears and are smaller than Oreos. Gary grabs one from the tank and drops it in my palms. I squeeze my arms together and watch the turtle waddle up the pale alley of skin, its claws tickling me gently. It's not a puppy, but it's so ugly that it's cute.

'I don't know,' Mom says. 'Turtles sound like a lot of work.'

'But they don't bark or need to be walked or anything,' I say. 'Do they bite people?'

'He may snap at you if he feels threatened,' Gary says, 'but you almost never see that. They're peaceful, usually. Not like those pretty angelfish. They're mean bastards when they fight.' Mom doesn't seem to notice when Gary swears.

The turtle yawns and looks up at me. 'Hello?' I say.

'He likes you,' Gary says. 'He knows you'll take good care of him.'

We pay for the turtle for a hundred years. I hold it outside on the steps in a plastic bag with water, while Gary and Mom drift around the store looking at tanks and filters and gravels. I hate waiting for Mom. She's always saying she'll just be a minute and then takes like eighty minutes. When I was little, back when Dad still lived at our house, she ran into a shop at the Santa Claus Village once and didn't come right back out like she said she was going to. Dad banged the steering wheel and said, 'Goddamnit! Your mother will never come out of that store!' I thought it was true and I cried until he made me get out of the car. Now I think I feel like Dad. I don't want to be in charge of the plastic bag and the turtle all by myself.

When Mom and I finally get back to the station wagon, the sun has made the car so hot that I burn my belly on the metal seatbelt.

'Whew! Watch that bag,' Mom says, rolling down her window and then lighting a cigarette. 'After spending sixty dollars, I'm not in the mood for turtle soup.'

'Was sixty a deal?' I ask.

Mom doesn't answer. Then after a moment she says, 'Cara, when you said that angelfish were gay, what did you mean?'

'I don't know. They sound girly. Like kittens and ponies and stuff.'

'It's an adult word,' Mom says. The way she says 'dult' makes me think of the back section of the video store.

'I know what it means,' I say. I jiggle the turtle in the bag and watch it bob up and down. 'But you said crap before.'

'You need to think before you just say things, Cara.'

'OK,' I say. I think about how Gary put his hand on Mom's shoulder. 'Do you think Gary is cute?'

'Oh for Christ's sake, don't change the topic,' Mom says. 'And stop moving that bag around. You'll make the turtle seasick.'

At home we have our passing party with cake and ice cream. Jed thinks the turtle is the best. We call him Ernie because he looks and moves like Ernie Sherman, the pharmacist where Mom buys her cigarettes because she won't run into anyone from Quit4Life. Mom says Jed gets to keep Ernie in his room since I got to pick him, but we're supposed to split playing fifty-fifty. Jed and I create obstacle courses for Ernie with old toilet paper rolls and Lego blocks. We talk about the junk inside his shell. We flood Mom's rock garden to build a mini-marsh that we call his 'natural habitat'. When Jed goes to hockey camp up north for a week, I bring Ernie's tank into my room and fall asleep to the sound of the filter, like water boiling softly.

When school starts again, I don't get to play with Ernie as much because Jed stops letting me in his room. He goes in there with his friend Toby every day after school to play records and ignore me. This means that Jed also doesn't help me with my maths homework like Mom made him promise, so I am terrified that I'll fail or get moved into the retard room.

After thanksgiving we have a maths quiz on fractions and I can't remember how to put the numbers together. Everyone around me is scratching things down super fast and it's like a race where I'm the slowest. I look at what Valerie is doing to my right, but her arm is covering her paper so I can't see. Valerie Calorie. That's what we call her because she is fat. She also thinks she is the smartest person in the world and whenever she explains anything, she sighs really loud and talks with her eyes half closed so that you can see the purple veins in her lids. She already has boobs, but not in the way that is cool.

I stare at the blank page and remember Mrs Arsenault, our teacher, saying something about fractions being like a pie that you cut into pieces. I draw a circle at the top of my page and cut some lines through it. I don't understand why we have to learn about broken numbers. If something is broken, it's wrecked and useless anyway. If it's not your fault that it's broken, you usually don't need to care about it.

'Two minutes,' Mrs Arsenault says. I stare hard at the pie, hoping I'll remember what I'm supposed to do with the pieces. I draw some more lines. Then I attach a little neck, a small head and some feet. I draw a little flower for Ernie to eat. Then Mrs Arsenault says to trade our papers for grading. I take Valerie Calorie's from her, but I don't give her mine.

'What's your problem?' she says, hands on her hips.

'Nothing, what's yours?'

'You're supposed to give me that!' She tries to grab my paper from me but I hold it down with my fist. She pulls harder and it rips in two. She gets the chunk with the picture of Ernie and she laughs with her mouth open wide. 'You are the one with the problem,' she says. 'You're retarded.'

I grab the black magic marker from inside my desk and swipe it across her yellow sweater. She squeals like a little pig and knocks back her chair. I put the tip of the marker on my own sweater and draw a faint line so I can say she attacked me first, but Mrs Arsenault sees me do it.

I get sent to see Mrs Burgess, the new principal with the powdery face. She is away at a dentist appointment, which is lucky, but the secretary makes me stay anyway. She gives me a piece of foolscap and tells me to write a letter of apology to Valerie. She doesn't care that Valerie said I was retarded. She smokes a cigarette and laughs on the phone while I sit across from her, waiting for the bell to ring. I can't think of anything to write to Valerie except that she should be more like a fraction and get skinnier.

'You didn't get very far,' the secretary says when the bell finally rings. 'Not too bright. Now you'll have to do it for homework.'

After school I jump whenever the phone rings because it might be Mrs Calorie or Mrs Arsenault calling Mom to complain about me. I sit on my bed and try writing the letter. I write: Dear Valerie, I'm sorry I got mad today and drew on you. I shouldn't have done it. I hope we can still be friends. The last part is definitely a lie, but I think Mrs Arsenault will like it. I decide to ask Jed what he thinks. He'll at least think it's cool that I got in trouble. He got sent to Mrs Burgess last week for poking little pins through the skin on his fingertips and chasing after Mandy Marsh, who does actually have cool boobs.

I can hear music coming from Jed's room down the hall. I open the door a crack and see Jed and Toby looking down at the record player. Jed is holding Ernie over the turntable. He puts him down shell-first and then puts his index finger on his belly.

'Watch this, he'll go flying,' Jed says.

I look at Ernie's tiny, twitching legs and I feel like I'm going to be sick. 'Don't do it, Jed!' I say. 'You'll hurt him.'

Jed looks up at me, hair hanging over his eyes. 'Private property,' he says.

'You're being mean,' I say.

'Don't be so gay,' Toby says. 'Turtles don't feel anything. They have shells.'

'Don't make references to people's sexual preferences,' I say. Toby squints at me like it's the stupidest thing he ever heard anyone say.

'Ignore her,' Jed tells Toby. 'She's a retard.'

'He's my turtle too,' I say.

Jed turns up the volume on Montego Bay and takes his finger off Ernie's pale yellow belly. Ernie spins around slowly at first and then faster when Jed flips the player to chipmunk-speed. I watch Ernie drift closer and closer to the edge of the record. My heart is beating super fast like in this dream I have sometimes where I'm standing on the edge of a high diving board and some crazy guy is climbing up behind me. If I say anything though, I'm afraid I'll start to cry. After a few seconds, Ernie zips off the turntable, flies over the record needle and lands on his feet on Jed's bed. Thank you God, I whisper in my head.

'Fuckin' A!' Toby says. Jed picks Ernie up off the bed and Toby slams the door.

I'm still standing in the hallway when Mom comes around to tell Jed and Toby to get ready for hockey practice. She asks me if I want to come along with them and have hot chocolate, but I don't want to go. Now that I'm ten, she lets me stay home by myself for up to an hour.

This is important, because I need to save Ernie.

After they leave, I go back to Jed's room. It smells like dirty laundry and vinegar and I have to step around the records on the floor to get to Ernie's tank. Ernie is sleeping on a big plastic rock.

'Hey there, Ern,' I say. 'I'm sorry that Jed's mean now.' Ernie jumps from his rock and swims down to the gravel. Black-brown slime is all over the glass and it gets on the sleeve of my sweater when I reach in to pick him up.

'I'm going to save you, OK?' I say. 'I am going to tell Mom what Jed did and how your tank's all sick.' I put Ernie on the palm of my hand and spread my fingers out. He is almost as big as my whole hand now. I stroke Ernie's shell with my fingers, tracing his lines. When my fingers get close to his head, he opens up his mouth really wide like he's going to yawn and then he chomps at the air. I jump backwards like Valerie Calorie and Ernie flips up off my palm and crashes off the edge of the tank and onto the floor. I wait to see if he will move, but nothing happens.

Ernie has never snapped before. Jed has turned him nasty. I look at Ernie on the floor and I'm afraid to touch him. I poke his shell gently with my toe, but he stays completely still. My heart starts banging again.

'Come on out, Ernie. You're OK,' I say. I kneel down and scrape him up with one of Jed's records. His legs wiggle a little, but his head stays scrunched in. I slide Ernie off the record, back into the tank. He doggy paddles with one arm, but his left side dips underwater. I pick him up carefully and drop him on the rock where he'd been sleeping.

'Just stay there,' I whisper. I close the tank and leave the bedroom as fast and controlled as I can. Please let Ernie be OK. Please let Ernie be OK.

Back in my room, I pick up my note to Valerie Calorie. When I read it again, I notice that the printing looks sideways and stupid. Mrs Arsenault always says my printing is clumsy. I rip up the letter. Rip it up into tinier and tinier pieces until it's like snow covering my comforter. When I hear the slam of the car door outside, I throw all of the pieces under my bed.

I don't see Ernie dead. Jed finds him. I can hear Mom in the hall telling Jed that it was probably an infection that killed Ernie. 'You took good care of him, sweetheart,' she says. 'These things happen.'

Mom says there is sad news and asks me to come down to the kitchen to talk with her and Jed. While she explains about Ernie, Jed keeps his eyes on me. I don't say anything to either of them.

'Did you notice anything unusual about Ernie?' Mom asks. 'Anything that was different today or yesterday?'

'I don't know,' I say. Jed's neck and ears are bright pink. He thinks I'm going to tell. He thinks it was his fault.

Mom asks if we want to have a funeral for Ernie or do anything to say goodbye. We both say no. She takes the chocolate ice cream out of the freezer and scoops out two large bowls.

'Well,' she says, 'someone I know has a birthday coming up.' She tugs my ponytail. 'You both loved Ernie. Should we start to talk about another kind of pet?'

Jed and I both stare at our melting bowls of chocolate ice cream. When the phone rings, Mom waits a few seconds and then goes to answer it. If it's Mrs Calorie or Mrs Arsenault, I really don't care.

Safia Shah

Safia Shah lives in Casablanca, Morocco with her husband and two young children, having fled Spitalfields, East London. They used to have a deli selling traditional British foods: now they have ducks and seven baby tortoises. Safia is an uneasy porridge of Anglo/Indian/Afghan/Scottish. Needless to say she is highly opinionated but makes a mean clootie dumpling. Born into a family of writers, she admits that she forgot to concentrate at school and so became a TV news producer. She's worked with Afghan refugees in Pakistan, has practically starved to death in Germany and spent years in Paris, pretending to perfect her French.

Brown Bag

The bag did not look like the sort of luggage that causes a fuss: the kind of baggage that gets taken off a plane. It was nondescript, saggy, Tigger sticker peeling from one corner. Colourless. An everyday tote, a come-as-you-are-bag. Not a look-at-me bag. The ground crew thought so too. They tossed it unheeding into the frontloading section of their vehicle: zippy, go-anywhere-fast truck.

A passenger detained by the police: his belongings offloaded did not impress. Keeping the plane and passengers on the runway for 43 minutes: Mickey Mouse, minor, minute, insignificant. Sally says I was born without natural intelligence.

After they took Mum away, they returned her in an urn. They had cremated her at 980 degrees, Celsius. It had to be that hot to ensure adequate disintegration of her bodyparts. The new, portable nature of Mum got me thinking. I thought of Dennis and Sandra in Bournemouth. I thought they would not mind if we came to stay. When they had written in the guest book, to invite us, they had not specified the need for a body to be available in corporal form. I knew Mum was somewhere else, possibly already in Bournemouth. Perhaps she was with Dad and the School Caretaker and the Donut Girl from the arcade. Perhaps she was with Bernard Matthews or Michael Jackson. Dad must be waiting somewhere. Eighteen years is a long time to be lost.

When I had the yard sale, a man offered me 50p for my dresses, £1 for the telly and £2.50 for the couch. I took it but I knew he was a chancer.

The stranger in the check-in queue, who popped in ahead of me, was a chancer too. Suddenly, ahead in the queue, just like that. Not looking. No peripheral vision. The desk assistant pegged him out of the corner of her eye. No problem of perusal there. She gave a sort of 'humph', not a moan, or a groan but a swallowed sigh, a pillow-over-the-head-yawn. It was a comforting noise because it told me she did not approve of The Chancer.

Every now and then, he tapped his passport on the edge of her high desk. We, in the regular queue, knew she did not approve of his loitering and staring into the middle distance. We knew she would deal with him, effectively. When she caved and hurried him through, she could not meet my eye. She had fallen in my estimation. She drooped like that saggy little brown bag.

It was queue barging by the Donut Girl next: right after Mum. I could forgive The Caretaker because I could sense his daily fatigue before he died. The Donut Girl had no business jostling ahead like that. Unlike him, she had not worked hard, ending three years short of a gold watch and a caravanning retirement in Norfolk, dip, dunk, sprinkle and the occasional: 'D'you want sugar on that?' Nothing life-shortening. Dip, dunk, sprinkle, dip, dunk and sprinkle.

Mum must have known she was going. She had tidied her drawers. She had tidied her cupboards. She had even tidied her handbag. Mum was naturally messy. A naturally messy person with tidy drawers and cupboards indicates something.

Week-enders who rented the Cat-in-the-Hat-House, cartoon painted pink and green, commented on the abundance of our personal possessions left inside. Everything bulged with mismatch and ramshackle: old bikinis, holed wellies, half-bottles of fake tan. Many thought our food left in the fridge and the outside cats running wild 'homely'. We got some stars on TripAdvisor. Each time people came, we stayed at Sally's. Occasionally, we arrived home to a tidier house than when we had left. People felt included in our lives. From time to time, the week-enders left notes: even small gifts. 'I hope your girl grows up to be a credit to you.' Or 'I saw this and just thought of you. Love Nora'(who dropped the house key down the drain). None of the notes read: 'Sorry you'll not be alive next year.' 'Your time's nearly up.' 'Just the Donut Girl to go, then you.'

I guess Mum simply got fast tracked like Creepy Sam from the stockroom at ChickenLand. He was going places at high speed: whoosh; right to the top. He became a manager, even though we started the same day.

When Mr Baxter interviewed me for a position at ChickenLand, the counter was shiny and the buns were floppy. I applied for the night shift. Mr B and I sat on small pink plastic stools. His legs were almost touching mine. Mr B suggested I stroke his knees, to test my sandwich handling abilities. I guess I did okay because I got the job. I never saw Mr B making sandwiches. He used to walk behind us at that high counter, smoothing our uniforms. Mine needed additional crease removal, as it was too tight on the bottom and chest. It rode up at the back and down at the front. It had belonged to the chicken fryer before me. She had left old tissues in the left pocket and a hair clip in the right. Mr B let me take chicken crumbs home for the cats.

Soon after I was born, the midwife told Mum I was 'God's child; a special gift, given to a chosen womb.' We had a photo of my tiny head squashed to her brown bosom as it heaved in her navy dress. Mum did not act blessed, she acted silly. Once, she and Sally made me phone directory enquiries and when the woman asked me 'which name, please?', I said 'Jennifer Pritchard'. Mum and Sally rolled about and said the operator did not want to know my name. Then we were all laughing and Sally slipped in a spillage of gin and Mum said she was wetting her knickers. They went into her room after that and closed the door. I could hear them giggling for hours. It made me happy to lie on the stripped sofa in the Cat-in-the-Hat-House and listen to them whispering and chuckling behind the door.

When Sally was not at our place, Mum often slept on the sofa. Her hand would cradle her G and T like a teddy bear. Sometimes, I shuffled up on the floor and her hand would touch my head too, the ice slowly warming on my temple.

It had been easy preparing to go to meet Mum in The Queue For The Chosen: the yard sale, the Ebay auctions, the eHow site, trapping the cats under the stairs, but now there was this alarming wait. All the rushing around to get ready seemed wasted.

The Bournemouth trip was important: a sort of abstract queue barge. It might speed things up, hopefully at little inconvenience to others in line. Bournemouth was not far but it seemed important to fly.

When Social Services came around with a file marked: 'J Pritchard', they stressed the importance of a balanced diet. Then they saw my room. I collect pictures of people wearing rubber waders or aprons. Aprons one wall, waders the opposite wall. Social Services asked me why there were so many more pictures of aprons. Obviously, waders in pictorial form are harder to come by. Sally once suggested that I expanded the waders category to include rubber in general. Mum told her to leave me alone. Rubber is too lumpy. Surprisingly, the one thing the week-enders never commented upon was my pictures. They rearranged them, though, because the Blu-TacK never matched up to how it had been before they arrived.

When Mum changed form, I first thought I should live with Sally but she came to give people sandwiches and drinks and to take back a green crop top Mum had got from her dress swap. Then she closed herself out of the Cat-in-the-Hat-House, forever.Instead of living with Sally, I stared out of the back window because Mum once told me you can spot people's faces in flames and panes. I did spot someone's face: the woman living across the road.

Each night, the woman sat in her kitchen and stared at me. Sometimes she flapped her arms. Sometimes she pointed to the ceiling. Once she shook her head. I flapped and danced back. I looked forward to our conversations.

After a few weeks, the leaves grew on the bushes outside the window and I could not see the woman anymore. She dropped in a note. I hoped it was an invitation to live with her but it said: 'You have a wasp's nest on your roof.'

After that, I thought Mum and I might as well go and wait for my turn to be called with Dennis and Sandra in Bournemouth.

I was reassured that nobody would mess with Mum's remains during our trip. eHow said: 'Under no circumstances is security allowed to open the urn to check the contents.' It was easy to buy the ticket because I am skilled in the use of automated booking systems. Dad was skilled in the handling of cutlery. He used to favour spoons, Mum says. I find myself treating the spoons very kindly too. Sometimes I worry that the knives and forks will take offence but I just cannot help myself, the spoons are spoilt and get washed first. From time to time, I sneak the other cutlery out of the drawer to wash it, just so it feels less left out. Dad got lost on holiday and never came back to the Cat-in-the-Hat-House. Mum said she had last seen him with cases and a palm tree on his shirt. That was shortly after the midwife clutched me to her chest. Mum says she looked for him but he must have missed his return flight because he never made it back. Maybe he was the first in the queue: waiting with The Caretaker, the Donut Girl, Bernard Matthews and Michael Jackson.

Although I liked Mum's new transportable shape, I missed her smell. Every now and then, when she had been in the bathroom and it was all foggy and warm, I would lock myself in and inhale that steam. It smelled of soap and quinine and gin and sweat. You could not get a comforting smell like that from an urn. I had a dream with a smell in it once. There was acetone in it and hair dye and drain cleaner, all lined up in bottles. They faded and then there was a young girl in a nightdress. She crept out of her hospital bed at dusk and found a tiny ginger kitten and a huge silver fish. She picked them up but the fish was too heavy and the kitten was too squirmy. It was getting really dark and sadly, she realised that she would have to go back to bed in the ward. She left them outside and tiptoed back. Nobody had noticed she was gone. She dreamt she had prepared a balanced meal all by herself. When I woke up, the bottles were lined up in my room but there was no sign of the girl or the fish or the kitten. My bed was wet. There was just me. Our cats locked under the stairs. Mum in her pot and the visitors' book open at the note from Dennis and Sandra: It read 'If you're ever in Dorset, pop in for tea.'

A dreary little bag: not a duffle, nor a tote, certainly not a case or a clutch. Just a bag shaped bag. If that bag ever did feature on the early evening news, surely it had a responsibility to appear noteworthy? Descript. A bag of distinction. Detailed enough to base an eyewitness account on.'The second I set eyes on that piece of luggage I just knew it was up to no good.' A bad-news-bag. An 'I-smell-a-rat-bag'. It oozed trouble.

Body parts on the ceiling. Fuselage blown to bits.

Urns are more reliable than little brown bags.

Melanie Whipman

Melanie Whipman has written stories for as long as she can remember. She grew up in Brighton, then travelled widely, working in all sorts of strange places – as an au pair, postwoman, interpreter, selling hair-transplants, picking avocados, painting dairies, cleaning waterslides and selling pharmaceuticals. She now lives in a leafy Surrey village with her husband and twelve year old twins. She has a first class BA in English and an MA (with distinction) in Creative Writing. Her short stories have been published in several magazines and her first novel, *Cadillac*, was long-listed in this year's Cinnamon Press Award. She teaches Creative Writing at Surrey County Council.

Baking Blind

It isn't how I imagined. There are three girls bunched up on the sofa; six pale knees in a row and five stilleto shoes scattered on the floor. One of the girls has the sixth in her hands and she's covering up the scuff marks with a black felt-tip. Three pairs of eyes flick between the scribbling pen and the television. They greeted me in English, a quick 'hi' as I stood in the living room doorway, but they are now back to their conversation, speaking in my language, but too low for me to make out all the words. Something about a party last night. One of the girls says an English phrase and the others laugh and repeat it. It's an odd phrase – it has the sort of sound that would make you smile, with a soft 'sp' and a 'b' and two words that almost rhyme. I don't know what it means. They laugh again and glance at me and the knot in my stomach gets tighter. It's crispy laughter, like my Mum's pies, the crust shiny and crackly, but when you dig deep it's pale and soggy inside. I let go of the door and step into the room, 'Do you know where Barute is?' I ask.

Barute said there'd be pork pies and fish and chips and shops stocked full of designer clothes and I'd see Hugh Grant and Liam Gallagher just walking along the street. I didn't let on, but he was wasting his breath – it was the sea I was going for. When Dad was alive he had a map of Britain on his classroom wall. He took me to work once, when I was off school with glandular fever and I couldn't take another day stuck at home with Mum. I sat at the back, swallowing my coughs as he spun out words I'd never heard. He was a different person there, he still spoke softly, but the English made his voice bigger and all the students listened to him. He'd taught me stuff at home, of course, read me English poems at bedtime, taught me how to count, but nothing like this. Mum used to tell him he was showing off. You make me feel stupid, she said. In the classroom he seemed to expand, you could feel the quiet certainty of him beneath every phrase. He was reading Shakespeare. I let his words flow round me as I stared at the poster on the wall, where Britain floated in a sea of blue, like a magic island. You'd feel safe there and free.

Barute was my step-dad's friend. 'Kas naujo?' he said, standing in our tiny kitchen in his flour-white shirt and shaking my Mum's hand as if she was important. I liked him, he never looked at me the way some men do, with that weight behind their eyes. He was flash – always had the latest phone and he drove a white BMW, with a fat spoiler, but he seemed comfortable here. No reason why he shouldn't, he was from the Lazdynai Estate too, a boy made good. His sister had gone to my school. Mum had spent all morning cleaning up the flat and had tried to make apple pyragas again. She's always been an awful cook, Dad and I used to laugh at her. She made a pie once and forgot to put the filling in, just the burnt crust and nothing inside. Barute ate his whole slice of pyraga, chewing and chewing the doughy pastry, nodding his appreciation as he washed it down with gulps of tea. I wanted to hug him.

'You've made the right decision,' he said, raising his voice above the traffic that filtered through the gaps in the flaking window putty. 'Fancy meeting the Queen?' And he ruffled my hair like I was six, not sixteen. Mum tugged at the hem of her best top and told him she was worried about the cost – surely renting my room out wouldn't cover the air fare. But Barute said I'd earn enough to pay him back in a month. 'Nieko tokio!' – 'no problem!' he said, laying a hand on the vee of flesh at the top of his crisp white shirt. I was a clever girl and thanks to my father my English was excellent.

'You should have seen them,' Mum said, 'closeted together for hours, I couldn't understand a word.'

'So her father's brains and your looks.'

She laughed, covering her mouth with the back of her hand in that gesture she has. Barute nodded and smiled. In England, he said, au pairs were paid a lot, but with my grades and my language skills, I could name my price. I'd send money home each month and my accent would improve so much, that when I came back I'd be able to walk straight into any university. He held his arms out either side of him – two doors opening wide.

It was my first time out of Lithuania and my first trip out of Vilnius since Dad died. My heart was knocking at the bottom of my throat as I took one last look at my bedroom. I'd pulled down the Oasis and Hamlet posters, packed away my soft toys and all my books. It looked strange and bare, as if I'd left long ago. Barute said it would be easier if Mum didn't come to the airport. He took my bag to the car while we said our goodbyes. My step-dad had already made himself scarce, another excuse to go down the pub.

'Bye then, Mum.' I touched her arm and turned to go, but she lunged towards me and hugged me tight like she used to do. Our bodies touched in the same places and her purr of laughter rumbled against my chest, 'You're as tall as me now. All grown up.' She pulled her head away and I could see the tears in the eyes. 'I always loved your Dad, you know that don't you?'

They'd met when Dad was a student. She worked as a waitress in a coffee shop down the road from Vilnius University. 'We used to all go down there, just to look at her,' Dad said, 'tongues hanging out, jaws on the floor, she was the most beautiful thing I'd ever seen. I couldn't believe it when she chose me.'

I stepped back from her and reached for the door.

'You do know that, Laima, don't you?'

She looked tired, there were scribbled lines at the corner of her eyes and faint brackets round her mouth. 'It's okay Mum, I know.'

I hoped some of my friends would see me in Barute's BMW as we drove down Savanoriu Street and over the sludgy curves of the River Neris. Barute told me what I'd need to say at the passport control in

England. A holiday visiting my cousins. His cygnet ring tap-tapped the bottom of the steering wheel as he pulled into the traffic heading out of Lazdynai. 'For an easy life, eh. And not a lie really, you'll be staying with some other Lithuanians first. Who's to say they're not long lost relatives?'

He wrote down the address for me and filled in the forms on the plane. The seats were narrow and we were snugged so close his elbow jogged against my side as he wrote. He'd given me the window seat, so I had nowhere to go when the warm length of his thigh pressed mine. He smelt of cedar and cigarettes when he leaned across me to slide in the seatbelt and when the engines roared and we left the ground he whispered in my ear, 'Nesijaudink. Don't worry, Goldilocks, they'll love you.' I could feel the hot huff of his breath through my hair and when his hand cupped my head, to bring me even closer, his finger slipped into my other ear, in and out, like it was an accident, but this time he was looking at me like I was sixteen, not six.

I was used to that look. 'I think I know your sister.' I said, shifting closer to the wall. Men are always hitting on me: boys at school, blokes in the street, in pubs, in the library, in the museum. Last winter a guy skiing in the Pasuka Parkas came up to me and asked me out for dinner. His breath steaming in the air and the two of us gloved and scarved and coated. I wondered what he saw. They all have that same heaviness behind their eyes. You have to get past it, make them see you're a real person. It's not difficult, you find something in common, anything non-sexual. The school kids are easy, you know their mother, or their brother or sister. You talk about family stuff. Strangers are more difficult, but you can usually tap into something. Since Mum remarried I practically live down the library. I'm there till the grey lady chucks me out. I'll read anything, so I know loads of useless facts. Like the coastline of Britain is 17,820 km and the furthest you can ever be from the sea is 113 km. The man in the park liked meteorology. He took me to the opera and then the

Krautevele. It was the best meal I'd ever had and we spent the whole evening talking about Baron Schilling and Rossby waves. He never laid a finger on me.

'I think I know your sister.' I said to Barute and then the air hostess shoved a tray at us and we were too busy opening plastic packets to talk.

My English stood up to the customs man. When I stepped across the yellow line he held out a hand, palm up, for my passport. I didn't show off, no Shakespeare to irritate him. I understood everything he said and when I spoke, my accent worked. 'Thank you, Sir.'

'Enjoy your holiday.' He smiled back at me.

'Thank you very much, Sir, I'm sure I will. I've been looking forward to seeing your wonderful island.'

Outside the terminal it was so bright with fake lights, you couldn't tell whether it was night or day. I took my first deep breath of English air, sniffed in dust and fumes and cigarettes. No salt. I thought you'd be able to smell the sea wherever you were in England. I'd imagined clean, salty air. I'd looked up the words in Dad's dictionary: saline, briny, sodium chloride. He took me to the Black Sea once. A winter's day where the sky and sea dissolved into each other. We skimmed pebbles and made drip people in the sand. When I licked my skin I tasted like a mermaid.

'You okay, Goldilocks?' Barute took my passport and we waited next to a group of huddled smokers under the sign of a smiling pink elephant. A black van pulled up and Barute stepped forward. He leaned on the passenger door, his head through the window, his words too low to catch. He chucked a thumb towards the rear and I clambered in. There were benches along each wall, like the ones we had in the school gym.

'About an hour,' he said, 'give or take.' He slammed the doors and went to sit in the front, while I had to hang on tight at the back in the dark. There were just the tin walls and a sports bag and a white jumper, with embroidered poppies, crumpled on the floor.

In his classroom Dad had the 'Full Works of Shakespeare.' They took up an entire shelf. I ran my fingers along their fat spines, playing at being blind as I found the indented titles. When he could no longer teach, he took one with him. Hamlet, his favourite. You'd have thought a dying man would have gone for one of the comedies, but Dad always liked to face his fears. Towards the end he asked me to read it to him. The beauty of Shakespeare, he said, was that he showed us how we were all the same. He got beneath the skin, through the crust of culture, kings and common men, to the real stuff inside, he nodded, thumping his chest and wheezing out his sighing, cancerous cough. I read to him for hours. I don't know if I pronounced it right, but I liked the sound and the rhythm reminded me of the steady shush-shush of the sea.

'Spunk bubble.' The girl in the short yellow dress says again.

I lean against the brown vinyl sofa. 'I don't know that phrase. What does it mean?'

They laugh their crispy laughs and turn their attention to the television. 'This'll help you. A few weeks of TV and your English'll be perfect.'

It's some sort of cookery show, a lady is frying onions, the rings are turning translucent in the butter, the camera pans in so you can see how the heat softens the edges.

'Are you going to be au pairs too?'

They avoid my eyes and reach for the cans of diet coke on the coffee table.

'Barute's got my mobile...' I gesture at the telephone in the corner of the room, 'D'you think...?'

'Doesn't work.'

She's lying, I've already heard it ring. The girl with the blue mascara and the waist-length hair shakes her head at me. 'Incoming calls only.'

In Lithuania they only do that if you haven't paid your bill. Perhaps Barute's been lying, maybe it's not so easy to get a job here. Maybe that's why he's vanished.

The rasp of a key in the lock falls into the silence, then there's bolts sliding and the slam of the front door. The girls down their cokes and push their hands into their hair, fluffing it out and cupping and smoothing the ends.

'Laima! Ruta! Come on.' It's an English voice, his accent strangles their names.

They shove their bare feet into their identical shoes. 'Good luck.' They touch the third girl on the shoulder, a flutter of fingers, then they push past me and are gone. The felt-pen girl is left on the sofa, sitting straight and still, with her shoe in her lap. Either side of her are damp marks where the plastic has stuck to their four moist thighs.

It was dusk when we arrived. They opened the van doors and the air folded in, soft and cool. We were in a street of terraced houses, just like you see in English films. My legs had gone to sleep and I stumbled as I stepped down. Barute took my arm. 'Thanks, I'm fine.' He didn't let go.

'Has your sister been to England?' I said. But he was talking to the other bloke and when he turned to look at me, there was no weight behind his eyes. Just emptiness. He changed his grip, tucked my arm through his, as if to keep me safe. It must have been raining earlier, the railings on the wall were blistered with droplets and you could see the street lights gleaming silver in the slick pavement. We walked towards one of the houses. I closed my eyes, inhaled deeply, no smell of sea.

Two men come for the other girl and this time there's no pie crust smile. She looks as if she'd like to say something, her mouth opens and then her hand slips up to cover her lips. The silk sleeve of her dress shifts down and for a second I see the inside of her arm, the pale tracery of lavender veins and the needle marks freckling the tender tickly bit in the inner dip of her elbow. It's just me and the TV chef now, she's got a nice face and capable, floury hands. She's rolling out pastry in deft, practised strokes, lifting the pastry across the rolling pin and into the tin. Round and round her fingers go, pushing it into the corners up to the edges, the dough pliable and unresisting. 'Firm but gentle,' she says. She neatens the edges with a sharp knife, twisting the tin round on her fingertips and slicing off the stuff escaping over the edge. She jabs with the fork, prick, prick; rows of puncture marks. 'Now,' she says, 'we bake it blind. In a hot oven.'

'You ready?' It's Barute in the doorway, my jacket over his arm.

My stomach turns, raw and sludgy. 'Where are we going?'

'You'll see.'

The TV chef opens the oven door and shoves in the pale pastry. Baking Blind. It's a funny phrase. Perhaps that's what's been wrong with my Mum's pies. All that time in the library and I never looked up recipes, never bothered to help her in the kitchen. I was always too much of a Daddy's girl, my head always stuck in some book. When I get home I'll tell her.

Peter Winder

Peter Winder has been writing short and medium length stories for pleasure for many years. The stories are usually based on everyday life and have a strong sense of place. He was born in London and this has influenced the setting and character of some of the stories, while others are inspired by his European travels. He has had stories shortlisted in a number of competitions.

National Gallery

Working on a computer can be tiring. It is important to have a supporting chair, be the right distance from the screen and to have a good keyboard. It is also important to take rest breaks. At 11.00 and 15.30 I get up and walk the long way around the office to the water dispenser. I fill a cup and drink it looking out of the window. The view into the office well is not very interesting, but it allows my eyes to focus on objects further away. At 13.00 I go to the rest room and eat my sandwiches. This usually takes about 13 minutes. Sometimes it is longer because people talk to me. When I have finished my lunch I go down the stairs to the entrance hall. There are eight floors with three flights of stairs between each floor so I go down twenty-four flights and twist through 2880 degrees. I could use the lift, but the exercise is good for me.

I turn left from the main door and walk directly along to Trafalgar Square. I cross on to the actual square, which is not really a square and walk through the tourists. I usually look up at Nelson and at the buskers. I don't like the fountains, but I don't have to go near them. I go up the steps and into the National Gallery, usually arriving about 13.29. I go through the main entrance and turn right into the Modern Gallery. I like the pictures in there. My favourites were both painted by Vincent Van Gogh, they are a picture of a chair and a picture of a wheat field. When my mother first suggested that I could look in the National Gallery in my lunch time I walked through the building trying to look at all the paintings, but there are over 2,300 pictures and I got confused. It is impossible to look at all of them. Now I always look at the pictures in the Modern Gallery. At 13.46 I leave the gallery and hope that there are not groups of tourists blocking the exit. As long as I hurry I get back to my desk by 14.00.

There are always other people in the modern gallery. In the summer sometimes there are lots of tourists and it is difficult to look at the pictures properly. There are other visitors who are not tourists. A thin, old man with white hair comes on Thursdays. He takes off his glasses and leans close to the pictures to look at them, which is strange. He looks at every picture. I don't think that he has favourites like me. Some days, there is a woman in a blue coat like a quilt, with shopping bags, she sits down and just gazes around. I don't think she looks at the paintings carefully.

On the 9th of June I noticed a young woman with blonde curly hair. I thought that I had seen her before. I remembered her because her hair looked artificial. It was almost white with dark near her head and blue patches, like ink on it. She was small and it was difficult to guess her age. She was looking at 'A Hillside in Provence' when I arrived. I saw her for two more days after that, but not every day. She seemed to have the same clothes, ordinary jeans and a pale blue tee shirt. They might have been different clothes that looked the same, but they were not very clean. When I saw her she was looking at the same picture or at other pictures by Cézanne. I know that he was very influential, but I prefer Van Gogh. When I stood next to her I noticed that she had three earrings through her left ear and she was smelly. I saw her two more times and the next day, Friday, she was with a young man with fluffy hair and a beard. She was showing him 'A Hillside in Provence'. He had his arm on her shoulder. She was nice-looking, but I would not like to have put my hand on her dirty tee-shirt. After that I didn't see her again.

On Sunday 22nd of June I saw something strange. Unless we go on an outing, my mother and I always watch the evening news on BBC1. We have a dish aerial that receives television from satellites and

I watch the news on lots of other news channels to find out about the rest of the world, but my mother says that BBC is best. There was news about a missing girl, Julie Stevens. She was seventeen. She had left her home in Sheffield to go to college and disappeared. Her mother was interviewed and said that her daughter wanted to go to art college and had never been in trouble and then she cried. There was a picture of Julie in school uniform. I thought that she looked like the woman I had seen in the National Gallery, but I couldn't be certain because of the different hair and clothes, also the girl in the school photo was smiling and the young woman in the gallery never looked happy. I told my mother. She said that it seemed unlikely that a young girl, missing in Sheffield, would appear in the National Gallery in London. I think that she realised that I was still worrying about this because, later, she said that if the girl had left home of her own free will and gone to London, then surely she would have sent a message to her mother telling her not to worry.

I thought that what my mother said was sensible, but perhaps the woman had seen the news item on television and realised that there was a police search and thought that she would get in a lot of trouble if she went back or even contacted her mother.

On Monday I did not eat my sandwiches so that I would have more time to look for the woman who might be Julie. She wasn't at the gallery and I was quite hungry. I ate my sandwiches on the train home. Missing Julie was not on the national news, but on one of the satellite channels where you can receive local news broadcasts. I went to a Yorkshire channel. As I had expected, they were still talking about the missing girl. Some girls from her college said that she had been unhappy because she had not managed to get a place at art school. One of them said that she was probably dressed like an ordinary person in jeans and that she looked different from the school photo. She said that Julie had white and blue hair and had three earrings in one ear.

I told my mother what the girls had said on television and that the woman I had seen must be the missing Julie. My mother looked worried. She said that she thought that it would be best if I continued to look for her and, if I saw her, tell the nearest policeman. I said that I could tell the police straight away and then they could search for her straight away.

Mum looked more worried and said, 'They wouldn't know where to look and I don't suppose that they could afford to have an officer guarding the gallery all the time.'

I didn't say any more because I did not want to worry her.

The next week I went to the gallery every day as normal, but I couldn't look at the pictures much because I was looking for Julie. I walked around all the galleries near the Modern Gallery and looked into the café. On Thursday I was hurrying back across the square because I was a little bit late, when I noticed a busker. At first I thought that he was just a regular busker and that I had seen him before, but when I had passed him I remembered where I had seen him. He had been the man with Julie in the gallery. I went straight back. He had just finished a song and a group of women tourists were putting money in his cap.

'Where is Julie Stevens,' I said.

He stared straight at me and I could see that he was thinking.

'Who?' he said.

'I saw you with Julie Stevens and she is a missing person.'

'I don't know what you're talking about. You must have the wrong person.'

I said, 'No. I saw you with her in the National Gallery.'

Then he gave me evidence that made me sure that he was lying. He said, 'I've never been in the building. You've got the wrong man.'

I knew that I had seen him. I had no doubt that he was the same person.

'I am going to tell the police,' I said.

As I turned to look around the square he looked much more worried. I thought that he might run away and that I would have to chase him. I was quite good at running at school, but it would have been embarrassing to run after him in London.

'Just a minute,' he said. 'You don't want to get her into a lot of trouble, do you?'

I didn't say anything.

'Come with me and I'll explain.'

I did not like this, but I thought that it was better than losing him or running after him.

He put his guitar in a case and picked up his hat and then started walking quite fast. I followed closely. I thought that he would suddenly run, but I think that he realised that I would be able to keep up with him. We went through a road beside the National Gallery and then turned left. At first I knew where we were, but then we went into small side streets that I did not know. Suddenly he turned into an alley between some tall buildings. It was only about one and a half metres wide and quite dark. He ran along the side of the building and turned left at the end of the alley behind it. I ran after him. As I ran round the corner he hit me with a piece of scaffold pole. I must have reacted very quickly, the way wild animals do, because I ducked sideways and covered my head with my arms. The pole missed my head and hit my left forearm very hard. I was shocked and just stared at him. I couldn't believe that he wanted to injure me. Then the pain made me scream. I felt like I had when I had been attacked by bullies at school. As he raised the pole again I jumped at him. My left hand wouldn't work properly, but I grabbed his face with my right hand. My thumb pulled up his lip and my little finger went in his eye. He screamed, dropped the pole and grabbed my wrist. I kicked his legs about four times. He tried to twist my wrist, but I kept on kicking his legs. When my toe hit his knee he groaned and fell over banging against my left arm. There was a lot more pain. I kept kicking him. I hurt so much I wanted to stamp on his head. Suddenly there were some men shouting at me and trying to grab me. They were wearing uniforms, but were not police officers. I thought that they were security men.

'Leave me alone,' I shouted, but I stopped kicking the busker.

One of them went to grab my arm, but stopped.

'Christ,' he said.

I saw that my arm was bent in the middle of the bone. I felt giddy and sat down.

They helped the busker up.

'What's this about?' one of them said.

'He attacked me. He's mad,' the busker said.

They all stared at me. I was feeling very ill.

'Don't let him go,' I said. 'Call the police about Julie Stevens.'

The busker started to walk back along the alley. I fainted.

I don't remember some of the rest that happened, but people have told me about it. They put me in an ambulance and a police woman managed to talk to me. I kept saying. 'Don't let him go. He knows where Julie Stevens is.' The security men didn't let the busker go until the police arrived. The police woman and her colleague arrested him on suspicion of causing me grievous bodily harm. The ambulance took me to hospital and the busker was taken to a police station. The police who had arrested him did not know who Julie Stevens was and he said that he had never heard of her and that I was mad. Eventually they found out who she was, I expect that they have a police intelligence network. When they asked him where he lived he said that he did not have a home, but lived rough. That means sleeping under bridges and places like that. They kept him at the police station and next morning came to see me in hospital. My radius bone was fractured in several places. I didn't feel well, the doctor said that that was because of the effects of the anaesthetic. I don't even remember this bit. The police officer asked me why the busker had hit me. I explained the whole thing to her and told her that I had seen Julie showing him 'Hillside in Provence'. This was important, because she went to the National Gallery and looked at their security video tape. Later she told me that the tape showed the busker standing with Julie. He said that he had met her when he was busking in the square, but didn't know her name. He said that lots of girls chat to him and he had forgotten that he had gone into the gallery with her to look at some pictures that interested her. The police woman said that she did not believe him, but there was not enough evidence to charge him with anything, except for assault on me. I thought that he should be prosecuted, but my Mum did not want me to be a witness. She said that there would be a lot of fuss with reporters and photographers. I wanted everyone to know the truth, but I wouldn't have liked talking to all those people. So the police released him.

When I was in hospital I thought that I might lose my job. I don't like applying for jobs. It was all right. I went back to work after a few weeks and everyone was very nice to me. I don't go into the Modern Gallery now, I go in the side entrance near the shop and look at 'Dutch Scenes of Everyday Life'.

Rachael Withers

Rachael Withers was inspired to start writing after accidentally kicking her host family's dog on a French exchange. She began her writing career with a short article in her school newspaper detailing all the embarrassing things she did while in France. After university Rachael lived in Japan for six years. She spent this time teaching English and writing various articles and short stories. She also learnt how to swear comprehensively in Japanese. Rachael is currently studying for the MA in Creative Writing at Birkbeck College, University of London.

The Klinefelter's Adventures: Chromosome of Havoc

1. You wake up feeling disorientated and afraid. You have been dreaming but, for the moment, the content of the dream eludes you. You are fully clothed. There is a plate of crusts in the bed with you.

a) Turn over and go back to sleep. Go to 2.

b) Get up. Go to 3.

2. You are dreaming again; at least, you think it's a dream. In the dream David Shrigley, in the form of one of his own drawings, comes towards you carrying a cardboard box. He gives you the box. You open it. It contains pretty little bits of sparkling light. This, David Shrigley tells you, is hand-eye coordination. The bits swarm towards your hand, climb up your arm and then jump into your mouth. They taste like Pepsi-Max. They sound like the chirping of a baby bird. The chirping gets louder. You realise your alarm has been ringing for some time. Shit. You are late for college.

a) It's all too much. Feeling overwhelmed you turn over and go back to sleep. Go to 1.

b) Get up. Go to 3.

3. At this point it would be a good idea to look down at what you are wearing. Check carefully for holes, food stains and pen leaks.

a) You realise that your outfit features at least one of the above. You need to change. Go back to the beginning of 3.

b) All your clothes are clean! Go to 4.

c) If you have checked and had to change more than six times, you are now very, very late. Give up and go straight to 6.

4. You finish eating breakfast and are now suffused with a calm feeling and a distinct lack of your usual morning paranoia. Your mother, who is redecorating the kitchen an ill-advised shade of puce, asks you to measure something just by looking at it. Do not ask why she finds this ability of yours so miraculous. Look at the object in question – on this occasion a doorframe – and tell her how tall it is.

Note: You can only work in metric. People requiring measurements in feet and inches are doomed to disappointment.

a) The doorframe is 2 metres tall. Now leave the house and catch the bus to college. Go to 5.

b) The doorframe is 1.9 metres tall. Go to 3.

c) You are not a human ruler For God's Sake. Get annoyed. Tell her to leave you alone, then follow her up the stairs, shouting until an argument is in full swing. After half an hour, realise that you are extremely late. Grab your bag and run to the bus stop. Go to 6.

5. There is an old lady sitting across the aisle from you on the bus. She is wearing a maroon overcoat with tortoiseshell buttons and even from a distance of a few metres (2.65 to be exact) you can smell her odour of mothballs and boiled cabbage. She appears to be staring at you with grim determination, occasionally shaking her head slowly from side to side and grimacing.

a) If you missed breakfast and were not bestowed with the Impervious Shield Of Self-Confidence, decide that she is staring at you and spend the rest of the journey trying to work out what is wrong with you. Go to 8.

b) If you ate breakfast and were bestowed with the Impervious Shield Of Self-Confidence, decide she is not staring at you. Go to 7.

6. You are late and have missed the bus. You will have to catch the next bus and miss the beginning of your lecture. This makes you very anxious. Fretting, you try to remember not to speak out loud to yourself whilst in public. If you forget this rule people will stare in horror, think you are mad and change their seat on the bus to avoid you. Mothers will regard you with suspicion and pull their small

children close. The elderly will tremble.

a) You realise you have been speaking out loud. Go to 5.

b) You weren't speaking out loud, but in the process of checking now you are. Go to 5.

c) You haven't said anything out loud at all. Go to 7.

7. You arrive at college. The lecture is long and dull but afterwards some friends invite you to the pub. They are meeting in the Crown at 7pm tonight.

a) Smile and say you'd love to see them there. They invite you to come to the canteen for lunch. Go to 9.

b) You are worried that Evil Starvin Marvin, your skinny, acne-faced arch-enemy, 1.8 metres tall, might be there and try to make your life a misery. You say maybe, you'll Think About It. They say See You Later and you worry that maybe the way you said that you'd Think About It was a bit rude. Go to 10.

8. You arrive at college really panicking about being so late. You see Evil Starvin Marvin, your skinny, acne-faced arch-enemy, 1.8 metres tall, ahead of you in the corridor. Bugger. He will try to do something to make your life a misery. Beautiful Jennie, 1.75 metres tall and The Love Of Your Life, is also there, chatting to him and looking beautiful. Buggery bugger. As you approach, Marvin reaches into the uber-cool record bag slung over his shoulder and rummages. He suddenly throws a box of HB pencils all over the floor in front of you. 'So, how many pencils are there on the floor?' He taunts. 'N-n-n-ninety eight? N-n-n-ninety nine? I forbid you to pass until you've picked them all up and counted them.'

a) You bend down to pick up the pencils. Marvin kicks at them and knocks your fingers with his trainers in a way that is actually quite painful. He says 'Oh my God, I was only joking, I didn't realise you were THAT RETARDED.' You straighten up and slump off down the corridor. Go to 10.

b) A couple of people from your lecture group are even later than you and luckily choose that moment to come up behind you in the corridor. Marvin moves out of the way. You follow them, noticing with some satisfaction Marvin's pencils splintering into dust underfoot. IN YOUR DEEP-PAN, STUFFED-CRUST PIZZA-FACE, MARVIN, IN YOUR FACE, (you think to yourself). You turn and look over your shoulder at the carnage of stationery like the Duke of Cumberland surveying Culloden Moor: Victory! Go to your lecture and then go to 9.

9. Lunch at college. Having lunch with your friends, you have to decide between the vegetable lasagne or the fish and chips. You are not good at making decisions.

a) You pick the lasagne. It's not very nice. Eat half and then throw the rest away. You promise to meet your mates in the pub later. Go to 11.

b) You pick the fish and chips. It's really good. Eat nearly all of it. Go to 10.

c) You really can't decide. It takes you ten minutes to choose the fish and chips, but by then there's no fish left. You take away a horrid looking portion of vegetable lasagne. One of your mates calls it Foetus On A Plate. You can't eat it. Leave the canteen. Go to 12.

10. Your mobile rings. It says Number Withheld. Answer the phone. Bear in mind if the person on the other end starts talking without saying hello or introducing themselves properly, it is probably your sister. On the other hand it could be some kind of dangerous mentalist. The person on the other end starts talking without saying hello or introducing themselves properly. Wait till they have finished their sentence then take action.

a) If you suspect it is a dangerous mentalist calling, hang up immediately. Go to 1.

b) If you decide it is your sister looking for relationship advice (Why is she asking you? She must be in real trouble) say, 'I'm sorry I really can't talk now,' hang up and go to 11.

c) If you are prepared to risk staying on the phone, despite being uncertain of the caller, you will eventually find out it is the hospital reminding you of your appointment with the endocrinologist this afternoon. Go to 12.

11. As you are in the process of walking through campus, a girl, 1.6 metres tall, asks you to sign her petition campaigning for the rights of Palestinians. She gives you a biro and asks you to Make Your Mark on the line. This is an unfamiliar expression and you're not quite sure what she means by it. She did ask you to sign it first, but does that mean the same as Make Your Mark? Unusual language constructions often flummox you. She is quite pretty as well. How embarrassing.

a) If you ate breakfast and were bestowed with the Impervious Shield Of Self-Confidence ask her if she wants you to sign the petition. She laughs, looks a little confused, then says 'Er, yes, of course' and points to the box. You sign. Go to 12.

b) If you did not have breakfast, but did experience the David Shrigley dream in which you received the gift of hand-eye co-ordination, twirl the pen around your finger expertly. Feeling a bit more comfortable with yourself, explain that you have a form of autism and don't understand exactly what she means. She looks at you with a combination of pity and embarrassment, says she's so sorry for troubling you, smiles, then walks off. Maybe she wasn't that pretty after all. Go to 12.

c) If you missed out on the David Shrigley dream, breakfast and eating the delicious fish and chips lunch, then that is just typical. It's sod's law really. You look at the girl, but genuinely have no idea what to do next. You lower your eyes, examining the interesting logo across the front of her tee-shirt. It looks like the Coca-Cola logo, but instead of saying 'Drink Coke' it says 'Destroy Capitalism'. It's quite clever. You have been staring for rather a long time now. You hope she will realise you have problems with language processing and helps you. You look up. The expression on her face is possibly anger. 'I can tell you're staring at my tits, Pervert!' She storms off. Go to 13.

12. You arrive at the endocrinologist's office in time for your appointment. He is a pleasant German man, 1.85 metres tall, with

an interesting moustache. The ends curl up a bit like a half-hearted handlebar. You would have expected that as a German he would have steered away from the whole unusual moustache area. You decide against bringing it up in conversation.

The Doctor asks how the testosterone treatment is going. You say it helps with the mood swings. He smiles and asks if you are interested in having a bone scan to check for osteoporosis. You have a greatly increased risk of developing this as you get older, due to your naturally low level of testosterone.

a) Say yes. Make an appointment for next week. Go to 14.

b) Say you think waiting for the results will be too stressful for you. Go to 13.

13. Have you brushed your teeth today? Probably... or maybe not. Have you brushed your teeth?

a) If you think you have go to 14.

b) If you can't remember, worry about it for a while then go to 15.

14. You go to the Crown, Beautiful Jennie, 1.75 metres tall and The Love Of Your Life is there. She starts to chat to you at the bar while you are ordering a drink. It's going well. In the process of conversation you mention your visit to the endocrinologist. She asks why you see an endocrinologist and you explain that you have Klinefelter's Syndrome. You refer to it humourously as making you:

a) part woman. You have used this chat-up line before and it has never been known to induce anything but loathing in ladies. You wish you hadn't said anything. Go to 17

b) a superhero: one of the XXY men. She doesn't understand, but she laughs anyway. Go to 16.

15. But was that memory of brushing your teeth actually from yesterday?

a) If you remember it WAS yesterday go to 16.

b) If you're still not sure, worry about it for a while and then go to 16 anyway.

16. Part way through the conversation you realise you have been

talking about yourself a lot and you may not have asked Beautiful Jennie 'How Are You?' Normal people always begin conversations with 'How Are You?' This is a rule of conversation. Think back over what you have said so far. Have you asked 'How Are You?' If the answer is no, it may be necessary to stop the conversation and enquire after her health.

a) You think you did say it somewhere near the beginning. Proceed with the conversation. Go to 17.

b) No, you didn't. Stop everything, ask 'How Are You?' then go to 18.

17. Evil Starvin Marvin enters the pub. 'Oi, Rainman!' You tense. Beautiful Jennie notices. 'You left me with my stuff all over the floor, you're supposed to be my mate. That means you owe me a drink. That's what a mate would do.' 'Don't be such a Dick, Marvin.' This is Jennie, The Love Of Your Life speaking – wonderful, beautiful, confident Jennie. She is 1.75 metres tall – the perfect height. She is the most perfect creature in the entire world. Marvin leaves you alone.

a) A lump of intense emotion rises in your throat. You ask her out. Go to 19.

b) You say thank you quietly and then ask if she would like a drink. Go to 18.

18. Buy a pint of lager for yourself and a gin and tonic for Beautiful Jennie, The Love Of Your Life. Take a thirsty sip.

a) If you have collected hand-eye coordination in a dream involving David Shrigley, successfully complete the manoeuvre. Go to 20.

b) If you have not encountered David Shrigley and the magical gift of hand-eye coordination, pour your pint down your front instead of into your mouth. Jennie, The Love Of Your Life laughs. You laugh. Then she says, 'You're really cute,' we should go out on a date some time. Things like this never happen to you. You say yes. THE END

19. Beautiful Jennie, The Love Of Your Life, explains that Marvin is still her boyfriend. She's really sorry that he's been so horrible, but he gets really jealous of her male friends. It's just because he loves her

so much. You consider vomiting all over her, but in the end settle for taking another sip of the lager of despair. THE END

20. You look at Beautiful Jennie, The Love Of Your Life. You ask if she would like to go out to dinner with you.

a) If you decided that the door frame was 1.9 metres tall this morning, then she says yes! Hooray! THE END

b) If you decided that the doorframe was 2 metres tall this morning, then look down and realise that there is a curry stain on your trousers. Jennie looks at it and smiles. Go to 19.

c) If you missed breakfast and the Impervious Shield Of Self-Confidence, don't give her time to reply. Say you were only joking and change the subject quickly. Phew, that was close. You nearly humiliated yourself. THE END

THE ACTUAL END

Acknowledgments

Many thanks to the following for their very generous help and support with this year's Bristol Short Story Prize:

Our readers – Katherine Hanks, Lu Hersey, Richard Jones, Mike Manson, Dawn Pomroy, Ali Reynolds and Keith Taylor; this year's judges – Bertel Martin (chair), Joe Berger, Maia Bristol, Helen Hart and Tania Hershman; Arts Council England; Chris Hill, Jonathan Ward, Claire Shorrock and the 3rd year Illustration students at University of the West of England; and Peter Begen, Joe Burt, Funky Dog, Mark Furneval, Ellen Grant, Fran Ham, Mel Harris at Waterstone's, Nicky Johns, Sylvie Kruiniger, Marc Leverton, Kathy McDermott, Natasha Melia, Peter Morgan, Dave Oakley, John Sansom, Joe Spurgeon & Venue Magazine and, most importantly, to all the writers who sent in their wonderful stories.